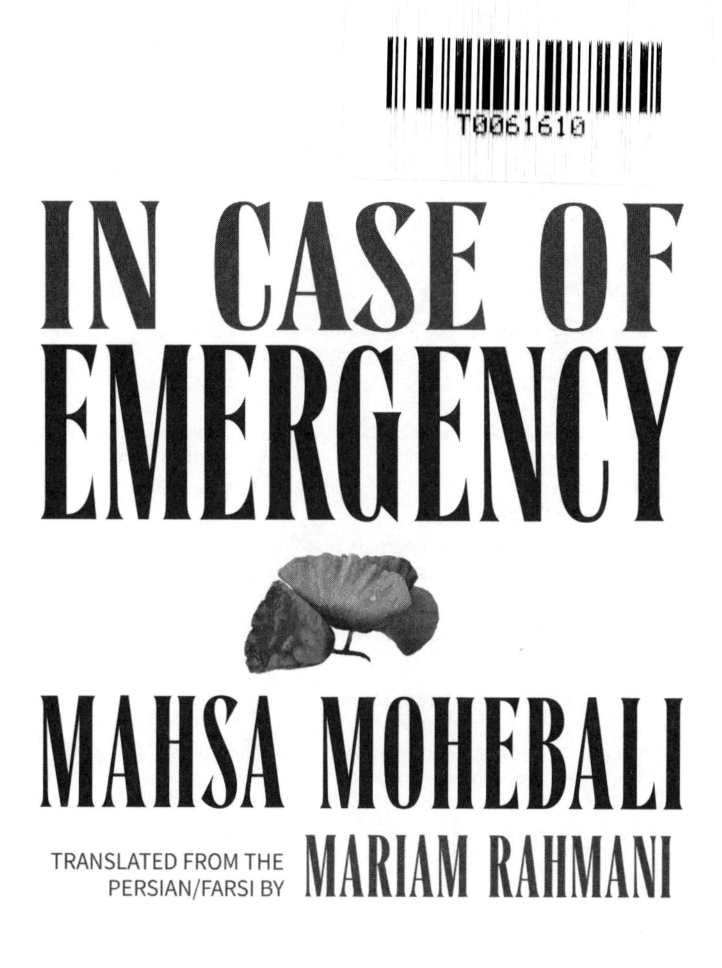

IN CASE OF EMERGENCY

MAHSA MOHEBALI

TRANSLATED FROM THE PERSIAN/FARSI BY MARIAM RAHMANI

THE FEMINIST PRESS
AT THE CITY UNIVERSITY OF NEW YORK
NEW YORK CITY

Published in 2021 by the Feminist Press
at the City University of New York
The Graduate Center
365 Fifth Avenue, Suite 5406
New York, NY 10016

feministpress.org

First Feminist Press edition 2021

The translator would like to thank the PEN/Heim Translation Fund Grant, Bread Loaf Translators' Conference Scholarship (made possible with funding from the Katharine Bakeless Nason Endowment), and the American Literary Translators Association's Jansen Fellowship for support.

This book was made possible thanks to a grant from the New York State Council on the Arts with the support of the Governor and the New York State Legislature.

This book is supported in part by an award from the National Endowment for the Arts.

First printing November 2021

Cover design by Sharanya Durvasula
Text design by Drew Stevens

Library of Congress Cataloging-in-Publication Data
Names: Mohebali, Mahsa, author. | Rahmani, Mariam, translator.
Title: In case of emergency / Mahsa Mohebali ; translated from the Persian/Farsi by Mariam Rahmani.
Other titles: Nigarān nabāsh. English
Description: First Feminist Press edition. | New York City : Feminist Press, 2021. | English translation of Farsi-Persian novel.
Identifiers: LCCN 2021032870 (print) | LCCN 2021032871 (ebook) | ISBN 9781952177866 (paperback) | ISBN 9781952177873 (ebook)
Subjects: LCSH: Tehran (Iran)--Fiction. | LCGFT: Apocalyptic fiction.
Classification: LCC PK6562.23.O44 N5413 2021 (print) | LCC PK6562.23.O44 (ebook) | DDC 891/.5534--dc23
LC record available at https://lccn.loc.gov/2021032870
LC ebook record available at https://lccn.loc.gov/2021032871

PRINTED IN THE UNITED STATES OF AMERICA

IN CASE OF EMERGENCY

IN CASE OF EMERGENCY

C*lick-click*, she's right by my ear. I can't move. If she sees I'm awake, she won't leave. She whispers and clicks. Clicks. Clicks till she hits a thousand or two and the digital prayer beads go off. The beeping announces that she's prayed enough to absolve us all of our sins. Or not.

She probably hasn't put the thing down since midnight, when the tremors started. She opened the door and screamed every half hour. Screaming bloody murder ten times for each tremor: How many screams does that make?

They were all yelling and screaming till the sun came up. Baba's voice was the only one missing. I bet he didn't even move a muscle, like during the night bombings back in the day.

I haven't moved either. I mean, I was high all night. And I floated even higher every time the bed caught a wave. Like a boat or maybe a cradle. Or no, like a coffin. That's what it is now, a coffin stuffed with wet sheets. If I can just stay still . . . Her whispers start to recede. This would make for a sweet high-angle shot—me facedown on a pillow in jeans and a sweaty T-shirt, all twisted up in wrinkled sheets. Why is this comedown so fucking bad? Her whispers get closer.

"Rise and shine, darling." *Click*.

They don't yell at me anymore, not since they found me up a tree like some fucking frog.

"Everyone's ready to go, and your father will be here any minute." *Click*.

She's trying so damn hard to be nice.

"The same thing happened in Bam. At first it was tremors, and then the big one." *Click*.

Good, this is good. Try to stay calm, just like that.

"Those bastards." *Click*. "For god's sake, get up. Ya abolfazl—"

"Ya abolfazl" and her screams merge with the *clitter-clatter* of the windowpanes. The bed catches a wave, slides in and out. She throws herself on top of me. It makes my skin crawl. She digs her nails into my arms. She screams. The *thump-thump* coming from Arash's room cuts out. Bobak sprints upstairs so he can kneel by the bed and hold her. Now she can extract her nails from my biceps and throw herself in his arms instead, scream in his ears instead.

Arash's sublime voice wafts in across the upstairs parlor.

"Siiiick. Hell yeah."

The windows stop trembling. The bed's caught its last wave. Except the prayer beads and necklaces hanging from the mirror keep swaying. I clutch the matchbox tucked under my pillow and turn over. Maman lies in Bobak's arms, a frail body in a Nike tracksuit. He whispers in her ear.

"It's over, Maman, it's over . . . Baba will get here any minute now."

"This shithole is about to collapse under our feet. We'll be buried here in the end."

She's sobbing. Bobak takes her by the armpits and lifts her like a piece of antique china. And like a sparrow she trembles in his arms. So this is what's become of the self-proclaimed guerrilla who used to pass out samizdat and trek through switchbacks packing a gun?

"Goddamn this shithole!"

"We'll head out any minute now, Maman, any minute . . ."

I shut my eyes and mutter, "Shut the door."

Bobak turns to look at me over his shoulder. Sadly. Or no, actually more like sadly and beseechingly. A Jean Reno kind of look, the kind of look nobody else knows how to give. As if to say, *Shadi, today of all days the least you could do is lay off the crazy.* Or maybe, *Shadi, think of Maman for once.* Which he doesn't say. He shuts the door.

I open the bottle. Only six left. As in a day and a half. What if Siamak's clean out of supplies? Or Rahim's gone missing in the shitstorm outside? Fool, don't even go there. Always remember Newton's First Law: Think not when coming down for thou thinkst out of thine ass.

And don't worry about the Second Law; when you're high it all works out in the end.

I place an opium ball under my tongue and suck on the bitterness.

"Are you waiting for the sky to fall?"

Maman is standing in the doorway, bellowing with such rich bass that it sounds nothing like her. Isn't she forgetting she's not supposed to yell at me? I close my eyes and turn to face the wall.

"The whole city's emptying out, haven't you noticed? Does the sky have to fall?"

She can drop a couple octaves and keep belting it out just like a bona fide prima donna. I suck on the bitterness. A little creature sets out from the lowest vertebra of my spine, calmly crawls up, then hurls itself from my neck into my skull. My mind goes blank. Blanker than blank. Something drips from inside me. Miss Gelin's cries sail up from the first floor.

"Mrs. Hardadi?" she calls for her mistress.

Where's Nana Molouk gone this time? *Thump-thump* spills out of Arash's room. Maman's probably standing in his doorway now, delivering the rest of her aria to an accompaniment of heavy metal.

"They'll cut off the water, they'll cut off the electricity, they'll cut off the gas, there won't be anyone left in town. Get up and—"

The sound of something hitting the doorframe cuts her off. Must be Arash throwing a slipper or shoe at the stage per usual. A few moments of silence and she launches into the finale: she stands at the center of the parlor, throws her head back, and wails. What a shame, all that depth and range wasted on disciplining her kids. Cue the crescendo: "I'll be digging my own grave because of you two, digging my own grave . . ."

She beats her head with both hands. Well, not exactly. Or at least not hard enough to mess up her coiffure.

Bobak comes in hot and calms her down. He's always ruining the show right before the climax. This bitch has some crazy mojo. How *does* he do it, calm her down just like that? I suck at the bitterness and swallow my spit. And decrescendo: "I'm tired, you've tired me out . . . Bobak, call your father and tell him to come deal with them. I actually don't give a damn what he does with himself. But my kids are coming with me."

On the decrescendo her voice loses all that grand depth. Back to the usual whining. Bobak whispers something. I can't hear what but the effect is wonderful, water on fire. I keep sucking. The bitter sludge under my tongue melts some more.

Bobak hovers in the doorway, giving me that Jean Reno heartbreaker look again. I want to tell him something: *Boy, with those eyes of yours, it's like you were made to slay.*

"So you're not getting up?"

He's wearing khakis by Paco Rabanne and a tee by Giordano in "ecru," which complements his silky chestnut hair terribly well. All prim and proper on a day like this. When did you even find time to shower? At midnight when everybody was all twisted up screaming for mercy?

Bobak stands over me, hands in his pockets.

"Can't you see Maman's worried about you?"

I close my eyes.

"Don't you care?"

One hand's playing with his keys. The little creature slowly crawls down my spine, then hurls itself into my pelvis. Again something drips from inside me. I suck and swallow the bitterness that melts off.

"We have to stick together. What if something happens?"

He looks at me sadly. Look, boy, you gave it your all. Tried to keep the family together, carried your mother in a palanquin. But now it's time to fuck off. I don't have the patience for you anymore. I want to lie right here until another thousand earthquakes hit and the roof rains down on me and all the bricks and beams fall down and crush me. And it's nobody else's goddamn business.

I shut my eyes.

"Get lost."

Finally I hear him leave. I open my eyes. Sure enough, Bobak's not standing there over my head. The sound of the TV floods in. That asshole left the door open. Zia Atabay's going crazy live from LA while Miss Gelin's laments rise from the first floor like a heartbreaking Japanese love song: "Mrs. Hardadi?"

"Shut up, you old hag!"

That would be Arash. Troubling himself, no doubt, to bend over the railing and holler at the maid while scratching at the fuzz on his chest. Soon he's whistling

"O Fortuna," and then there's the sound of him taking a piss, like holding a hose over a swimming pool. Unclear whether the man whistles when he needs a piss or whether he needs a piss when he whistles.

"Shut the door to the can!" Maman screams.

Arash cracks up and keeps humming "O Fortuna."

Now he's at the door still scratching at his furry body. It's a wonder how Maman ever gave birth to that. I mean Bobak and me, I can see us packed in there one way or another, but this one? Nah.

"How's it going, bitch?"

He's got this jackal-jawed smile slapped on his face.

"Dude, these fucking quakes! You digging that Bandari beat? Shit, the internet is blow . . . ing . . . up."

"Where's Nana Molouk?" I ask.

"She already split. By now she's out there shaking it in one of Maman's ball gowns from Paris."

He holds out his arms, stands on his tiptoes, perks his ass, and sashays out the door.

"Where's Baba?" I call.

His head pops back through the doorframe.

"In the ninth circle of hell."

"Turn that fucking thing off, will you."

"Why? The strings just snapped on this city and Zia Darling's explaining why."

"Shut the door."

"Okay, okay, live a little!"

He shuts the door. The necklaces and prayer beads on the mirror tremble. Everything's looking a little jankier after last night. I swallow the bitterness. The little creature busts a gut trying to scale my spine. And what if I don't find Rahim or Siamak? Stop freaking out, you dumbass. Siamak's glued to that fucking stone age torch at Sara's place. An earthquake's nothing—his ass wouldn't budge if an atom bomb hit this town.

Beep beep beep!

It's destiny knocking at the door. Where is that damn phone anyway? Whatever. I'm not in the mood for texts. It's always the same shit on repeat. *Have you heard from Rahim?* for example, like I'm her boyfriend's keeper.

Then there's Sara's relationship drama. *Do you think Siamak loves me?*

Or Ali's. *Do you know where Nilufar is?*

Or Elham's usual. *Have you heard from Mazyar?* Or Payam or Mohammad Reza or Hamed or a thousand other fools . . . To quote Mazyar himself, the poor girl has suffered from an acute dick deficiency for years.

Or maybe it's Baba pausing to think of his daughter amid all that—platonic, of course—flirting with his students.

"Mrs. Hardadi?"

Why is it that no one knows where Nana Molouk is?

Bet she woke up this morning only to realize she had a soiree on the calendar and nothing to wear, then after spending a good half hour looking for the keys to her Benz (without finding either the keys or the Benz) she figured she could use the walk, and now she's lost in the alleyways of Qolhak searching for Tajrish Square.

Bobak sprints upstairs again two by two. Then he

bumps his way back down, dragging Maman's suitcases step by step.

"Did he pick up the goddamn phone?" she calls after him.

"No one's answering the office phone and his cell goes straight to voicemail," Bobak yells up the stairs.

"Well if he's not at the office then where is he?"

"I'll try again in a sec!"

Bobak keeps hitting redial as he loads the suitcases into the car with the phone cradled against his shoulder. Go ahead, call him. Call him a thousand times. Or at least pretend like you're calling him. You should know by now that he won't pick up until all his staff's and students' emotional and spiritual problems are resolved. Or maybe you don't.

I shut my eyes and swallow the last bitter dregs under my tongue. The little creature crawls up my legs and hurls itself into my stomach. Now it breaks into a thousand pieces. The pieces in my stomach shift and leak into my legs, swim through my veins like tadpoles, go downstream and pull themselves back up to throw themselves into my pelvis, all thousand of them spilling into a single swamp. And now they're in my stomach swimming laps.

Beep!

Where is that goddamn phone? Please god, let it be under the bed. Thank god, for once it's exactly where I thought. Tiny hearts spill out of the message box. I hit the Okay button. It's Ashkan. I hit Okay again: "I can't stand it anymore. Goodbye." No! Not today, Ashkan.

How many times have you said goodbye? How many times have you thrown back forty Valiums and freaked everyone the fuck out? You can't stand what anymore exactly? Can't you just wait for this earthquake to fucking end you. Tell me something, why is it always forty? Just for once, try a hundred, two hundred, maybe more. Man up!

"Nah, dude, what the fuck are you talking about? You swear? Shit, dude. Kudos to them . . ."

Arash's friends can get a rise out of him any day, today must be a walk in the park. Ten to one they're planning to meet up at Mohseni Square like it's game night. Any second now his head's about to pop through the doorframe to say that everyone on Orkut's posted when and where. What for? To celebrate the city's good vibrations?

There's something stuck at the bottom of my throat. Stream's blocked. I need a cup of tea to get the tadpoles swimming again. To get them to come back up. Up into my mouth, up the back of my throat, and into my skull. Then I'll be able to think.

I yank the twisted sheet off me. How long will it last, this eternal battle between me and the linens? Is it possible for me to sleep a single night without turning over a thousand times like a rotisserie chicken? Hopefully this time Ashkan's decided to kill himself with opium instead of Valium. If Parvin actually wanted to stop him from getting hold of her shit, she'd stop tinkering with that damn lock on the medicine cabinet and buy a fucking safe. What if he swiped a solid twenty-five grams? My reflection in the mirror would do for a gnarly close-up of a mental patient: short spiky hair, jaundiced face, dark circles as black as bruises.

A bomb's gone off in the parlor. Pajamas and pantyhose and unpaired shoes are practically hanging from the ceiling. Arash's snickering has morphed into a cackle.

"Nah, dude! You're shitting me."

The wooden stairs creak under my feet. This spiral staircase is Nana Molouk's crown jewel, and it's popping like popcorn. Maybe in an hour, maybe in a day, maybe any minute now—with the Bandari beat the earth's got going, I wouldn't be surprised if it collapsed right under my feet.

Miss Gelin is sitting in the middle of the downstairs parlor, muttering under her breath. The second I put my foot on the last step she lifts her big, wet eyes to ask, "Mrs. Hardadi? Niyə mənə özünən aparmiyip?"

Her bag's on the floor beside her, and she clutches a bundle to her chest. Where has her mistress gone? And why hasn't she taken her with her? On the TV screen the news anchor stands on Razi Bridge, smiling and gesturing to the tangle of cars below. Entreating people to keep calm and carry on, I bet. Miss Gelin locks eyes with me and cries, "Mrs. Hardadi?"

Like she's whispering some ancient prayer. If only I were riding a little higher, I'd sit down and give it to her straight. She clutches at my pant leg.

"İstəyirəm gedəm xanım yanına."

I sit down. She takes my hand.

"Sən bilursən xanım hara gedib?"

"The lady's gone after her love."

She looks at me with a blank stare. Like I'm putting her on.

"Ağa gəlib de?"

"The lady's gone to find him."

She wipes her eyes with the corner of her scarf.

"Allah bilur!"

Fair, it's a little late for that. She should've gone for it when she had the chance.

Bobak comes over, phone in hand. I stare into his honeyed eyes. Bitch, how did you get so pretty? Too bad you're a mama's boy who won't cut the cord.

"Can you try giving Baba a call? Maman's having a heart attack."

I get up. Miss Gelin's still holding on to the hem of my pants.

"You know it's been medically proven that people who vent their emotions don't have heart attacks?"

"Shadi!"

He looks at me sadly now that he's yelled. Yes, dear, you must not yell at me. I am currently convalescing after the onset of a mental condition. How many times a day do I need to remind you people that I was found up in a tree just a few weeks ago? And as for now, I'm brain-dead before I have my cup of tea.

He chews on his lip and looks annoyed. He taps a heel on the floor.

"You wouldn't happen to have Ms. Vafaei's home phone number?"

I turn around and smile. Bravo! For once you've put that noggin to work. Where's Baba when he's not at his office? At Ms. Vafaei's or Ms. Malakouti's or Ms. Harandi's or . . . I mean, he's *some*where, at any rate.

"If it's not in the phone book—"

The ground gives out from under my feet. Miss Gelin screams. Bobak runs up the stairs two by two. Maman stands at the top of the stairs and screams. The crystal chandelier jingles and jangles. The news anchor tries to keep his balance. The camera pans on the sky. The image cuts out.

The tights won't go up my legs. Miss Gelin's got them back to front and she keeps twisting them around my legs. Bobak's combing his hair and I'm not even dressed yet. I start crying. Maman takes over.

Baba stands at the door checking his watch. Miss Gelin brushes my hair. Nana Molouk comes up the stairs.

"Are my little angels ready yet?"

She smiles at me. Maman lifts my skirt and pulls the tights up.

"It's late. They're children, not a circus act."

Baba strokes my hair and gives me a wink.

The downstairs parlor is full of people. Baba puts a hand on Bobak's back: "My eldest son, Bobak." Nana Molouk pushes me toward the old women: "My little princess."

My feet pedal backward. They stroke my hair with their wrinkled hands. Baba stands by the piano and taps a fork against his sour glass.

"My son and daughter have prepared a Paganini duet for you."

Everyone goes quiet. Somebody coughs. My father takes the violin out of the case for me. Nana Molouk smiles. Bobak sits at the piano and looks at me out of the corner of his eye. I lift the bow. My hands shake. Bobak whispers, "One, two, three, four."

I can't hear the violin. I simply shift my fingers and move the bow up and down. Bobak's fingers run up and down the keys. His hands don't shake. He glares at me. I'm messing it up. I'm messing it up. Nana Molouk smiles. Baba looks down at the glass he holds in front of his chest. I move the bow up and down. What am I doing? The sound of Maman laughing comes from somewhere. Nana Molouk follows it with her gaze. The kitchen door's ajar and Maman's skirt suit shows through the gap. There's a hand around her waist. She laughs again. Bobak glares. I move the bow back and forth. My fingers are freezing up. I can't hear a thing. Bobak's fingers run up and down the keys. I move the bow back and forth. I'm messing up. I'm messing up. My face gets hot. A puddle gathers at my feet. My eyes go blank.

Arash sits across from me with a head full of product. He's gelled it up like the crown of a hoopoe bird and now he's busy shoving pizza into his face. Cold pizza at this hour? Just thinking about it makes me sick. Mouth full, he's churning out manifestos as he chews: "This city's ours now, baby. All the motherfucking cowards are making a break for it."

I'm stretched out on the chaise downstairs, a tower of ash perched on the tip of my cigarette like the Leaning Tower of Pisa. Half the tower collapses before making it to the ashtray. I down the last swig of tea and slide the glass across the table. Bobak's shuttling from the kitchen to the car like some worker ant carrying basket after basket. Here's hoping he forgets to take that fresh thermos of tea. Maman's sitting by the door with a thumb to the keypad. Her scarf around her neck, digital prayer counter in hand. A thousand prayers to pardon our sins. She dials with one hand and click-clicks with the other. Mindlessly click-clicks without whispering any supplications. How's that supposed to work? At this rate we'll never reach salvation.

Arash stuffs another piece of cold pizza into his face. I want to hug him. I want to take that curly head of his between my hands, and I want to pinch his cheeks . . . I wish you'd never grown up. I wish you didn't have all that fuzz on your chest and cheeks and I wish I could swim with your arms clasped around my neck like old times. You never did learn how. Kind of like those report cards you ripped up on the way home from school so that Maman and Baba had to stand before principal and prefect with their heads bowed low to say, no indeed, they had not known that their son had failed several classes. Then there was the flute you didn't blow into once. And the French books you blew up after the first day of class. Better that than fucking it all up later, like me.

"Everything's ready to go."

Bobak's standing by Maman, brushing off his pants.

"They have to come too."

She isn't yelling anymore, she's whispering under her breath. Must be hatching some plan. Like what? What're you angling at now? You know that Baba's not about to spring into action. So why keep calling him? Just leave. And you know that we're not coming with you. At least you've got Bobak Dearest right there by your side. Don't forget to pack something nice in black, just in case you need to host our funerals out in Kelardasht. No need to come back for the bodies. Even if word is, the whole city's turned upside down. You can rest assured that we'll have been hit in the head by some brick or beam, swift mercy. Or maybe with a slight delay, a little pain, that's all. But me, I don't feel pain. Know that I'll be cresting a high when I give up the ghost. Just make it chic. Throw that black guipure scarf of yours over your wine-red hair, dab at the corners of your eyes, and say a few Fatihas for our souls.

Arash inhales the last piece of pizza. Good thing he takes breakfast into account when he orders dinner. He extracts a joint from pocket #1001 of his vest and lights it. Sucks the smoke in between cracked lips, holds his breath. Half the joint goes red. He hands it to me. I take a small puff and hand it back.

“Was that sad-ass hiccup supposed to be a fucking drag?”

I shut my eyes.

“What’s your problem, shove your pills up the wrong hole?”

I open my eyes. He’s got the joint between his thumb and forefinger, his neck’s bent back, and he’s taking a deep drag down to the bottom of his lungs. The front of his T-shirt announces, “The world’s best and biggest breakfast at the Intercontinental, Dubai & Abu Dhabi!” He looks at me with his Jezebel eyes.

Arash takes another drag and squints. Miss Gelin tiptoes over to the chaise and squats down next to it. Arash leans forward and whispers in my ear, “Tehroon’s banging out the Bandari to run them all out of town. All those fucking cowards and little shits.”

I procure a cigarette from pocket #1003.

“Then what?”

“*Then what?* Shit! Well then, the city is ours.”

I put the cigarette between my lips. Arash strikes the lighter. The flame spills out like a furnace. Miss Gelin shifts around. I take a deep breath and hold it in. Tastes like poison.

“And how are you so sure that all the fucking cowards and little shits won’t stick around?”

“Ha! Cowards don’t stick around, they split. Takes balls to stay.”

You plaster a big wide grin on your face and your Jezebel eyes brim with pure joy. I wish everything could be like this. Wish I’d been born a few years later, like you. Wish I'd gone to private school and a pricey second-rate college while dealing weed on the side. Then I'd be game. We'd head to Mohseni Square to set some wheels on fire and get in the trenches to take back a city that's popped off and started shaking it to Bandari without stopping to ask ourselves what the fuck we're doing.

"What time did the first earthquake hit?"

He leans forward and locks eyes with me.

"I don't know."

"Two thirty. Then what happened? The gods said 'fuck it' and went back to bed. What time did the second one hit? Five thirty. A few folks got scared and split. What time was the third? Quarter to eight. At that point some more pussies called it a wrap. The point is, she's warning them—pack up pronto, or else. Nothing's broken, not even a damn tea glass. These are all signs."

Miss Gelin clutches at the hem of her pants.

"Mrs. Hardadi?"

"You've got to be kidding me. Look, your lady's lost her fucking mind. Do you know what that means?"

Miss Gelin looks at him through wet eyes.

"Want me to take you?"

Miss Gelin looks at me. She wants to make sure he isn't trolling her.

"Should I put her on the back of my bike and let her go around Mohseni Square?" Arash asks.

I shut my eyes.

"You're really not feeling too hot, huh?"

"Go see if there's an old box of pastries or something in the fridge."

"Think you can find fucking pastries around here? Fuck this family. Bunch of barbarians. These fools don't understand a damn thing . . ."

His voice fades out by the time he reaches the kitchen. What am I going to do about Ashkan? Hopefully he tried killing himself with opium instead of Valium this time around. Shit. What if Parvin just bought a solid twenty-five grams? And Ashkan managed to break the lock or swipe the key?

"Don't ask me! They're coming with me and I don't care if I have to tie them up. I'm not going anywhere without my kids. You need to get yourself over here, pronto!"

Maman is yelling into the phone. Arash runs into the parlor and snatches it out of her hand.

"Shit, I'm not going anywhere. Tell your wife to fork over some cash."

He's holding a big box of koloocheh and a jar of plantain marmalade. Maman grabs the phone back.

"Khosrau, this house is falling to pieces right over our heads. Forget about that bumfuck university!"

Damn she screams a lot. Miss Gelin scuttles into the parlor. Bobak is standing by Maman, supposedly calming her down. So where was Baba after all?

Arash tosses me the food, cocks two finger guns at his hips, and drawls: "No one's going anywhere before you fork over some cash."

Maman shouts from across the room, "I'm not giving you a single sou. You can stay here and starve to death."

Arash smirks. Bobak takes the phone out of Maman's hand.

"Baba please, if you'd come—"

Maman snatches it back.

"Khosrau, I swear on your ancestors'—how the hell should I know where your mother is?"

Now that's the truth. Even General Afkhami himself can't fix this. Not this time. Forget about Intelligence or the police—they could send an army battalion searching today and they wouldn't find her. I put some elbow grease into it. The jar still won't open. Arash marches through the parlor whipping his belt around then stops to yell, loud enough for his voice to carry through the receiver, "Nobody leaves!"

"Khosrau!"

Now she's sobbing. Bobak takes the phone back from Maman and heads for the stairs. He sits on the third step and twitters into the mouthpiece. The dude spends all day whispering into the phone.

Bobak is on the phone, reasoning, negotiating, arguing, making logical deductions. Maman holds her head in her hands and lets the tears stream down. You look like a fucking joke in your tracksuit and sneakers. What dumbass told you that *that's* the dress code for disaster? Or what do I know, maybe a tracksuit will shield you against bricks and stones and steel beams. I suppose it's better than having to run out in a nightie with all the crazies on your tail. I give it another go. The jar still won't open.

"I'm not going anywhere. Running is for fucking cowards."

Arash sits in the middle of the parlor fiddling with our granddad's old hunting rifle. Where the hell did he get that from?

"Put that damn thing down."

Per usual Maman can't stand the sight of Nana Molouk's antique trash. I try again. The jar opens. I scoop a spoonful of the stuff onto my tongue. The marmalade mixes with my saliva and goes down. My stomach's starting to warm up. It's like the tadpoles have gotten a second wind. They swim up my esophagus and spill into my skull. My brain warms up. Bobak is still on the phone pleading. All of a sudden Maman dives in and grabs the receiver. Here comes a proper deluge of wifely swearing.

"Khosrau, I swear on my father's grave—"

And let the bawling begin. When you cry I can still see her in you—that girl from the provinces who escaped the arrests in the eighties by hiding out in her professor's house, then pushed out three kids for the kind, beloved professor only to forget about that whole guerrilla game so that her mother-in-law could traipse around clucking *shameless village girl*. Even now that Nana Molouk can't keep anyone or anything straight, she still says it sometimes.

After you're finished sobbing, you resume the screaming. For variety's sake, like the movements of a concerto. I eat another spoonful of marmalade. Arash has the butt of the rifle resting on his knee. He looks down the barrel, cool as a cucumber. Like some Texas blue blood who goes seven generations back. His jaw sags like John Wayne's: "Hand o'er the money."

I have to find Rahim. Siamak's not going anywhere but he's also as tight as a virgin. He acts like he'd rather kill himself than buy me drugs with my own money on a good day, and that's after skimming a full half off the top. It's either that or the genius plans to meet the dealer at the corner so when the authorities pop up he throws the shit in the gutter. But that's just the way of the world, right?

I dig my phone out of pocket #1005 and call Rahim. *All circuits are busy*. I dial up Siamak. *All circuits are busy*. I send Ashkan a text, "Be there in 5." *Message failed to send*. I send it again. *Message failed.* Send. Failed. Today is not my day. I try calling. *All circuits are busy*.

If all circuits weren't busy and Ashkan actually picked up the phone for once, I'd deliver a nice, calming lecture. So calming that he wouldn't try anything before I got there. Or no, scratch that. First thing I'd do is see whether we're talking opium or pills. God, I hope Parvin isn't home . . . Shit, a solid twenty-five grams could keep me high for what, five days? Ten? Surely somewhere in there a rogue brick or beam would knock me out cold and I'd mercifully meet my maker. I eat another spoonful of marmalade. Now this is how to do it right: eating stretched out with your food resting on your chest. Like you're eating in the grave. Arash comes over and shoves the spoon into his mouth. He tosses the gun from one hand to another and takes a koloocheh. It's not like he just polished off half a family-size pizza or anything.

"No bullshit. I'm talking cold, hard cash." He's

stuffed the koloocheh in his mouth whole and is talking through it.

Maman's on a new round of *click-clicking*. With the supplications. Better that than yelling and screaming. Miss Gelin scooches her butt back over to me. Please don't start. It's like she hears me. She clutches her bundle close to her chest and bows her head. Poor old woman. Nana Molouk's got miles of crazy but there's still no room for you in there? I call Rahim. *All circuits are busy*. I call again. And again. And again. It rings. And rings. And rings. He doesn't pick up.

"What's wrong, you sober?"

Arash is standing over my head looking at me with his maw open.

"Shut the fuck up."

"You fucking idiot. This place is flooded with drug dealers and you're out there chasing after that bitch's ass." He leans in and whispers, "Want me to sort you out? This shit's the real deal, I swear."

I don't open my eyes. There's the sound of him smacking his forehead with the palm of his hand.

"Oh right! I forgot you people don't fuck with pills. But seriously, bitch, can you actually end up in a tree just by messing around with a little opium?"

I crack up.

"Last call, sister. Think you can fool me."

I open my eyes so I can take a good look at those bushy eyebrows he likes to call Naser Malek Motiee–style all twisted up in a knot.

"Damn it feels good to make you feel bad."

"Inconceivable."

"Deal with it."

He wrings my neck.

"Profess your allegiance and join us."

I hit him in the head with a pillow. He throws himself into my arms and jabs at my stomach and biceps.

"Stop, you piece of shit, I can't breathe."

We fall off the chaise and roll onto the floor. Like when we were kids and he fit between my arms. Now I fit between his.

"Let her go. The child's half-dead as it is, she'll break something."

Maman's standing over us.

"Get up, both of you."

Arash gets up, picks up his gun, and starts following her around.

"Cold, hard cash."

I stretch out in the middle of the living room. The ceiling's full of cracks, and that prehistoric chandelier's hanging by a thread. I wish I could lie here and wait for its crystal tassels and tears to come crashing down. I wish they'd go already and leave me and the house and Nana Molouk alone. If only Nana Molouk hadn't left the house. I'd lie here and listen to her squeaky rocking chair. In peace and quiet. Nana Molouk is the only one who can sit by the window for hours without reading or crocheting or chatting or listening to music, just gazing into the courtyard.

"Give me that damn thing!"

Maman and Arash are at it again.

If the tremors had started in the afternoon, Nana Molouk and I would be sitting here right now, drinking tea and looking out at the oleander trees. Maman would be at the salon or in a boutique on Jordan Street or at lunch with the gang. And everyone else would be taking care of business, the daily grind. I need to go. I need to pull it together and go.

I take the stairs up two by two. Bobak slides his ass out of the way—those khakis mustn't get dirty. Maman and he both eye me suspiciously.

"Thank you, darling."

If I look at you to make you understand how idiotic you are, you'll take it from the top and start wailing from adagio to allegro. I throw my charger into my backpack. I pull open all the dresser drawers and turn them inside out. God knows, there might be a cigarette famine today too.

"Don't forget to pack a couple sweaters."

Bobak's standing by looking at me, this time with kind Jean Reno eyes. I miss him already. I go lock my hands around his neck. If Arash saw me he'd say, "Nah, looks like that was some quality shit."

Bobak's only a little taller than me. I press my forehead to his lips. Any other day he'd tell me I stink of smoke and booze and throw me in the shower. But today it's all gone to hell and I'm that precious baby sister you have to put up with even when she smells like shit. Who you've got to get to come with you, somehow, someway.

I stroke his cheek with the backs of my fingers. His skin's so velvety soft you'd never know he takes a razor to it every morning. Bobak fastens his pretty golden eyes to my eyes and smiles at me. I close my eyes and rest my head on his chest so he'll stroke it. His fingers run through my spiky hair.

"Psycho. Where's your suitcase?"

"Look, I've got a proposal. Forget about me for the day, how's that?"

"Where's your suitcase?"

I press myself into his arms.

He takes my face between his hands and looks at me sadly.

"Where's your suitcase?"

"Bobak! Do you even know how pretty you are?"

"Oof, Shadi, that's enough. Where's your suitcase?"

"It's not right. I mean, it's not fair. How come I didn't turn out like you?"

"Stop, seriously."

He pulls back.

"They had you during their lovey-dovey phase, proper family planning, but then when it came to me, well what can I say, and by the time Arash came around—I mean, now that was a royal fuckup. We're lucky they switched to separate bedrooms after that or we'd have a monkey on our hands by now."

Those amber eyes should be full of laughter, but they're not. You're worried. Worried about Maman, worried about Rose, worried about the business, worried about your employees, worried about Baba, worried about your shares, worried about your Xantia, worried about your presale apartment in Kaveh

Tower, worried about me. You peel me off you, take me by the shoulders, and squint to take a good look at me.

"Why are you being so nice?"

"It's the pills. On antidepressants you look like perfection."

"When are you going to ease off that stuff? You'll end up going insane."

"Insane? I'm already there. It's all genetics. You take all the shit genes on both sides of the family and add 'em up and you get me. There's Nana Molouk and Nayeb Asadollah on the paternal line, and on the maternal there's Umm Kulthum and Qubad Faizollah Beg and a whole bunch of other psychos . . . Hey, here's an idea, does committing identity theft fix your genetic makeup?"

Mozart's Sonata no. 1 swirls in through my ears. He lets go of my waist. It's his darling Rose calling.

"Yes, sweetheart?"

I shut the phone in his hand.

"Stop, crazy. It's Rose."

He hits the call-back button. I shut the phone in his hand again.

"Lucky Rose."

"Shadi, I swear, quit it. She's going to get worried."

Mozart spirals through my ears again. He removes my hands from his waist.

"Yeah, we got cut off. How are you? Uh-huh, we're getting ready to go. Okay, sweetheart. Okay, beautiful. Okay."

He shuts the phone. I sway from side to side with my hands clasped around his waist again.

"Remember how we used to play this sonata together? Well, how *you* used to play this sonata while I took a shit on it. Tell me something, were you faking it with all that whining or could you actually tell I was out of tune?"

The sound of something exploding mixes with glass shattering and someone screaming and a sweet whistling. Bobak disappears. The prince and his internet fiancée. I bend over the banister. Arash is standing in the middle of the living room with the gun, clapping for himself. Maman's glass buffet table has been reduced to a pile of dust on the floor. Miss Gelin's let go of her sorry sack so she can beat her head with two hands: "Allah bilur, Allah Allah . . ."

"How do you like them apples? Bull's-eye on the Belgian vase! Come on, honestly, check out that fucking aim."

Bobak grabs the barrel of the gun and yells.

"That's enough! Now you've really fucked up!"

Arash holds on.

"Careful, you'll get your hands dirty."

Bobak doesn't let go. Arash pulls the trigger. Due to Newton's Second Law, or maybe the Third, Bobak flies across the room. Arash takes aim at the sideboard over by the dining table.

"Think your baby bro can hit that thingy on the soup dish?"

Bobak rises like a wounded lion and levels Arash.

Bravo! Show us what you're made of, boy. They roll over. Bobak sits on Arash's chest and tries to wrestle the rifle out of his hands. He's stronger than Arash but he's got no technique. Now Bobak's back on the bottom and Arash has the rifle pointed at the base of his throat. He presses down. Clearly enjoying himself. He's got that Schwarzenegger feeling and the high is killing him.

"Let him go. Here's your money."

One- and two-thousand toman bills swirl in the air. There's the sound of Arash whistling and laughing. Of Bobak's shouts and Maman's screams. Of Miss Gelin's heartbreaking lament. I shut the door and collapse on my bed. I light a cigarette and take a drag. Bobak materializes in the doorway.

"Where's your suitcase?"

He's not messing around anymore. It's 0–1 against Arash and I'm going to be the one to pay.

"At the top of the closet, under the futons."

He yanks the closet door open. An avalanche of sweaters and CDs and books and bags and boots and papers tumbles over him like Mr. Whoopee. Bobak finds somewhere to plant his feet. With one hand he holds the stack of folded futons back, and with the other he tugs at the suitcase. Put your back into it. There, that's it! You can do it. He makes a real effort and the fine lines on his face scrunch up. Good! Let it out. You can't keep it bottled up forever. The futons hit him first, then the suitcase goes flying and he goes down with it.

Bobak puts the suitcase on the bed, opens it, and

turns around to see whether he can find anything useful in the mess expelled from the closet.

When will he finally give up this ridiculous charade? I ash my cigarette onto the floor. He doesn't look at me. He picks out a balled-up pair of jeans, folds them, and sets them in the suitcase. A light bulb goes off. Anything in reach gets folded and put in the suitcase. I should say something, but I can't be bothered. Why can't they understand that you don't set Arash off just to save some change? I take a deep breath.

"Arash goes out to collect like he's in the mob."

Bobak throws a button-up shirt into the suitcase.

"Does he think he's in Texas, sonofa—"

That's right, let it all out! You don't even know how good it makes you feel. Who knows how you ended up with all the good breeding this family has to offer.

"Texas shmexas, that's not the point," I say. "What I mean is, everyone has a different relationship to money."

"Right. Different."

He clutches a single sock as he searches for its mate. He'll never find it.

"Well take me, for example, for me money's for the finding. There's always a couple thousand somewhere. In Baba's pocket or Maman's coat pocket or your pants pocket or Arash's pants pocket . . . But Arash, he fights for it." You give up on the sock and stuff a gray T-shirt into the suitcase instead. "Not everyone has a knack for making money, like you do."

He won't look at me. He picks up another sock: fuchsia. The last one was yellow.

"Don't stress it. I'll wear them mismatched."

"What? Wear what mismatched?"

"Never mind."

The mere idea of wearing mismatched socks is beyond comprehension. He puts a pair of sneakers on top and shuts the suitcase.

"Get up. Baba's on his way, he'll be here any minute."

He drags the suitcase out without deigning to look at me. Once again the bed turns into a boat. The sound of Maman's screams and of Bobak's footsteps going down the stairs two by two. I shut my eyes. I want to sleep. Maman's moaning and wailing starts up again. The phone calls to Baba start up again. And the cycle repeats into eternity.

No. I have to get up. I have to go see Ashkan. I have to go see Sara. I have to go find Rahim or Siamak. Have to have to have to.

I put on my army jacket and pull my black beanie down to my eyebrows. I throw my backpack over my shoulder and look around the room. I wanted so badly to get crushed by your bricks and beams, but they just won't let that happen. Plus I need to get my hands on some shit. God knows, maybe I'll be back . . . Okay, yallah.

I creep down the spiral staircase. Maman's pacing out in the courtyard. Bobak is trying to fit my suitcase into the trunk of the car. The phone rings. It's sitting right by me, on the chaise. Maman launches herself into the parlor. I pick up the phone. Rose's smooth, sultry voice comes through.

"Shadi, dear, is that you?"

"Yes, babe, are you calling for—"

Maman grabs the phone out of my hand.

I step toward the door.

"Bobak, it's Rose!"

Bobak lets go of the suitcase and runs inside.

"Of course, darling," Maman says. "Just a moment, here he is."

Bobak takes the phone and starts his soft twittering. I slowly make it through the door.

"Where do you think you're going?"

Maman launches her aria into the courtyard. I open the gate and run. The street is packed. The trunks of the cars are all open and—I can hear Bobak shouting after me. Don't go back. Don't go back. The cars are bumper-to-bumper. I climb over them. Hood roof trunk hop, hood roof trunk . . . I hear Bobak. He shouts. Shouts. Shouts. He calls after me. Calls my name. I don't go back. I don't look back. I don't go back.

Shariati Street's packed. What are all these people even doing here? It's like everyone in the world's set up camp right here. Curses aimed at mothers and sisters spin through the air along with screams and shouts.

Some guy locks eyes with me. He heads straight over, looking like he can't wait to go off on me. Like someone you used to know who still leaves messages on the machine even though you never call back. I have no idea who he is. I keep walking. Deny all charges . . . My bad. He quietly passes me by.

A scrawny little kid with snot hanging off his nose and a mouth stretched big as a saucer comes up to me, stops, and screams. His parents come back—forgot the kid?—and glare at me like I owe them something. What, I'm not some auntie. I glare back. The father scoops him up. They get lost in the crowd.

I weave through the hordes. I stand on my tiptoes: just a shit ton of bodies and heads wiggling around. I won't be able see anything like this. If only I could find some kind of lookout to get my fill of the view. Maybe I still know how to scale a streetlight . . . Or better yet, there's that asinine fountain in the square—you can see everything from up there.

What jackass designed this monstrosity? I've asked myself the same damn question a thousand times. But what do I care? Some city employee has an epiphany one night in their sleep, or after chancing upon a Dalí sculpture one afternoon, thinks to fasten a few pipes together to render this piece of trash. Anyhow what matters is that you can sit on the horizontal pipes. No one's about to notice me perched up there cross-legged in the middle of this mess. I grab onto the pipes and climb. Hook my legs over and pull myself up like Léon the Professional. Down below there are a thousand cars tangled up in a knot. Some guy pushes through the crowd balancing an old chair on his head. Must be a family heirloom. I put my earbuds in and hit the Leave-It-to-Fate button on my MP3 player. I have yet to find the right soundtrack for this sort of scene.

"The road to happiness is under construction—"

This dude's already getting on my nerves. Pray tell, precisely which part of the road is under construction? I press the button again.

"One day you wake up to see it's you that's gone with the wind—"

Cry me a river, I feel like that every damn day.

Tom Waits's tired death rattle knocks around my head, silencing everything everywhere. Now that's more like it. I light a cigarette. Taking my time, I puff out smoke ring after smoke ring.

That sprawling accent and crossover voice draw me in, like I'm the one who's drunk and broke, sitting on the steps of the shrine at Imamzadeh Saleh warming my fingers with my breath just so I can write someone a letter, Arash or Sara or maybe even Bobak.

I start out just like that, writing of a child I have growing in my belly and the baby's kind father. I write that he drives a taxi and plays the setar and on Fridays we go to Farahzad for street corn. But my habit's bleeding me dry. With that kind of money I could buy me—well, not quite; around here you'd need more than dope money to buy yourself a used-car lot.

Some itsy-bitsy wisp of a woman has one hand gripped around a curtain rod and the other around the arm of an old lady who pants as she takes sparrow-small steps. Where are you taking the poor thing, wielding that scepter?

Some girl leans against the pole of the traffic light howling like a cheetah. Must be quoting prices, given those boys who've got their eyes glued on her. Every few minutes she raises a bottle to her plump lips and swigs till her cheeks bulge, and after that her mouth opens saddlebag big.

Tom Waits is the shit. That call-and-response between the piano and the vocals—just kills me every time. I take a drag, then watch the street through the smoke rings. Some guy with spiky hair gets out of a cherry-red Peugeot 206 and flaps about. This way, that way. His jaw drops. Up and down. He folds his hands on his head like the wretched of the earth. Looks around. Any second now and the waterworks start. A pretty woman carrying cocktail dresses fresh from the dry cleaner crashes into him as she elbows her way through the crowd.

The ATM's a beehive. A bunch of women in chadors claw at each other. I suppose the bearded guy standing there with his head bowed and eyes averted thinks he's doing something to help separate them. Another guy—bald, well-dressed, glasses—has his eyes trained on the ATM, one hand resting on his chest, calm and quiet as a guru. He'll go get some cash after this little siesta. So mindful. Like he could stand there in that same spot patiently waiting forever.

Why is everyone spinning in circles like a bunch of shit-dizzy flies? What difference does it make whether they wiggle a little this way or that way, it won't change what's happening underground . . . Or maybe it will. If Mazyar were here he'd say, *If you had a wife and three kids at home waiting for you to withdraw the rat turd's worth of savings you've managed to scrape together so you can take them someplace where the ground doesn't slip out from under your goddamn feet, then you'd be over here climbing over car hoods and stepping on people's heads too*. But what I want to know is, who asked them to breed in the first place? Take Behrouz Vossoughi's advice and hit 'em each on the head, one smack per mouth to feed. Now Tom Waits is at the part where the girl goes dancing with her husband on Saturday nights. She's in a thin pink dress, big floral print, hands clasped around her husband's waist as they spin through a room full of drunk couples.

A few of the guys crowded around Cheetah Girl with jackal-jawed smiles start trickling backward, which means she's unleashing a round of roadhouse curses. Her shoe goes up in the air next and she slinks down the pole, sits on the asphalt, and sets the bottle between her feet. The boys edge back toward her. The girl's mouth stretches big big big and—*whoosh* some beefcake swoops in and shoves one of the boys who falls back into the crowd and the rest of them disappear. Man takes girl by the arms and lifts her up. Girl slips back down. Man bends over and whispers something in her ear. Girl's mouth opens wide. Man whispers in her ear again. This time the bottle gets thrown in his face along with the requisite insults. Man backs away. Good to know this city's still got a person or two with a soupçon of self-respect.

This part of the song just doesn't do it for me. Poor Charley, why do I have to wake him from his sweet dream to slap him with the truth? I mean, who knows, maybe as I sit there sniveling over all that nonsense, an old friend will show up, someone loyal and decent who will see to the evening's debauchery. If it's Rahim, we'll sit together and let the wick of our memories burn. *Damn, Shadi! It all went too quick. Remember how we'd sit around Aqa Gholam's room, bless his fucking heart? Three hits and we'd hit the clouds. Those were the days.*

He'd probably even tear up like he always does. Such nostalgia. I can't. I take the cigarette butt, aim for the mindfulness guru and flick. It hits him on the back of his bald head, smack-dab in the middle. He touches the spot and looks around suspiciously like Johnny Dollar. I stick my tongue way out and lock eyes with him.

"It was me, over here!"

I point my thumb at my chest and plaster a big, wide grin across my face. He squints then tips down his glasses to get a good look at me. Surely he has to say something, swear at me, take a crack at me, *something* . . . Nothing. Seriously? He turns back around, hand glued to his chest, and starts staring at the ATM again. The guy's a proper Buddhist. Or something along those lines—he's concentrating on manifesting change with the power of his gaze, aiming to make the chadory women by the ATM calm down. Do your thing. I light another cigarette and watch him through the rings of smoke. Go ahead and give it your best shot. You've got till the end of this cigarette to achieve your Krishnamurtian feat or else I'm throwing this one at you too.

The pipes start to shake and a fresh set of screams tumble into the atmosphere. I fall straight on my ass, feet up. I stretch out. Open my arms. The sky sways back and forth and I'm lying on the ground nailed to the cross. The earth shudders and the shudders ripple through my body. They start at my fingertips and run through my shoulders and groin and damn! Let the Bandari begin. Mother Earth must be down there shimmying her big meaty breasts. The tremors speak to me.

Speak to me. Speak to me. I feel like it's my first time ever lying on the grass. I suckle at its scent. The earth settles down, a pause in a long sentence. I close my eyes, walk my fingers through the grass. Smells like rain. The smell of wetness, the smell of trees. I wish I could sink, pour into the earth and dance with her. Let the tremors crawl through my body. I don't want them to stop. I want to lie right here on this grass forever sucking on its wetness. I want my breasts to shiver with her shivers and make waves.

There's a guy sitting near me on his knees. He prostrates and tears slip down his cheeks. He's praying, imploring from the bottom of the bottom of his heart. Poor guy probably thinks the earth's dancing on account of his sins alone. I wish I could think the world were moving because of me. Just for me.

I climb the fountain again. Shariati's a mess; it looks like someone pulled the tablecloth out from under the place settings. People are taking shots at one another left and right. Yelling and screaming—I'll pass. I hit Leave-It-to-Fate.

"Stop, world, stop—I want to get off."

An answer to the devil's prayer . . . I hit the button again anyway.

"Someone's in the water surrendering the soul."

I'm sure it's Ashkan's spirit calling out to me. I must be the most cowardly little bitch the world's ever seen. But I don't want to go, I want to stay here and watch the crowds. Ashkan, you asshole. Isn't it a shame to kill yourself on a day as perfect as this?

"*Someone's in the water squandering their soul, rest in peace.*"

Why do I have to go check on him? No way I'm feeling guilty. Isn't Parvin the one who birthed the damn child? So Ashkan feels like letting the curtain drop on this earthly realm, how is that our problem?

An old woman dunks her head in the fountain beneath my feet and stays there. Hope she's not drowning. Why won't she take her head out of the water? Oh hell. Get up or you'll drown! Whatever, not my problem . . . She lifts her head and exhales with a big sigh and takes a seat right there. An old man brandishing both hands in the air walks over and yells at her. The woman keeps her eyes shut and shakes her head from side to side.

"*Someone in the water calls out your name, rest in peace.*"

Fuck it, Elham can go deal with him. What's it got to do with me?

Prince Peugeot's duking it out with a big guy in a bad suit who could pass for a bouncer. The bastard's throwing punches left and right. Prince Peugeot takes out a steering wheel lock and smashes the windshield of the bouncer's Xantia to smithereens. His wife stands by, clawing at her face.

"*He cries out hoping for help.*"

I was the one who took him to the hospital last time, the time before that Arash made it over there before he'd managed to set the house on fire, and the time before *that*—well, I can't remember. The point is, it's not my turn. Besides, where the hell is Elham in the middle of this shitstorm? Can you actually hook a rich bachelor on doomsday? And what about Parvin? Running circles around the city trying to find her old compadres, I bet.

"*Someone, someone within reach.*"

How many times has this kid tried killing himself? Instead of repeating my famous speech about how fucking lame the world is, I'm going to lecture him Siamak-style this time. The method involves taking a seat, looking Ashkan straight in the eyes, and educating. *Scientists have recently proven that love is nothing more than the rise and fall of hormone levels in the blood and, thus, has nothing whatsoever to do with emotions. Depression, in turn, is but a symptom of love*. And so on and so forth.

A frizzy-haired fat woman in a translucent white nightgown totters around beating herself on the head. A bald man runs after her yelling. Woman shakes her head from side to side and huffs and puffs. Man grabs onto her chubby arms and shakes. Woman collapses onto the lawn right by my feet. Her jaw drops, her face goes red, she clutches at her frizzy hair. She pulls out a chunk of hair and sets it on her lap, screams, then pulls out another chunk. Give it another ten minutes and she's bald.

"*Mouth open, eyes carved with fear, rest in peace.*"

A suicide attempt produces a state of steady stagnation in a person that effects a prolonged period in which one can listen to all kinds of bullshit without a peep of protest, that's the silver lining.

"*Calling from waters far or waters close, rest in peace.*"

How great is that, having it logically proven to you

that anyone in your shoes would be just as depressed as you are and pine after their beloved just like you do.

"*How shall I say it, when?*"

But someone is surrendering the soul—goddamn you, Ashkan. I take one last look at the most handsome street in Tehran. I may never see you looking so beautiful again. Cheetah Girl's head hangs low. Okay, okay, someone is surrendering the soul. Oh Shariati, my sincere regrets.

I want to skip all the way to the bridge. To get to Ashkan's as fast as I can so I can stop him from throwing back a solid twenty-five grams. What a waste. I hit Leave-It-to-Fate and this time fate has me spinning to the batshit beat of Arabic-Hindi-Russian fusion.

I step forward, I step back. I bump into someone. A woman turns around and frowns, mutters something under her breath. I twirl. Go ahead, say it! Curse all you want. Insult my mother, my sister, the whole family tree.

"*Someone is surrendering the soul, rest in peace.*"

I skip. Nobody's watching. Not even that boy with the nice dark features. Go ahead, look at me—what're the odds you'll ever see someone as crazy as me?

I spin around the streetlight, I swing from its bar.

"*Quilted with dew, the garden's green unfurls a prayer rug.*"

I spin around. One step forward, two steps back. I spin and crash into some guy's big fat belly, who gives me a look. I spin, I skip.

"*Someone within reach, rest in peace.*"

I prance dance bounce. Crash. This time a little boy

falls down. I pick him up. He's not out here alone, is he? The kid's mother arrives and pulls him by the hand.

"Make a Mecca of any direction, rest in peace."

I wrap my arms around the pole. I skip spin come face-to-face with some guy with a bad sunburn. He flashes a jackal-jawed smile. I smile at him and skip away. Even if he follows me there's no way he'll find me.

"Someone is surrendering the soul."

I skip. I spin.

"Someone who wants a word with you, rest in peace."

I spin. I take two steps back.

"Make a Mecca—"

I skip. Nobody's watching. I spin.

"Quilted with dew . . ."

As I turn off the main street, a bloodcurdling cry drills into my skull. A tiny tongue pokes out of a beet-red face—I can't believe this little rascal is the source of all that noise. The kid's mother is dressed in an orange manteau, rocking the stroller back and forth. Oblivious to the shrieking. A robot set on automatic, she pushes and pulls with one hand while punching numbers into her phone with the other. If cell towers could talk, they'd be cursing our fathers and our fathers' fathers by now. The baby sticks four wet fingers in his mouth, reaching all the way back. How long has he been screaming?

They must have woken him up during the first tremors and brought him out here. The mother's nightgown pokes out from under her manteau. She missed a couple buttons this morning and the left side's shorter by a handspan. Crooked clothes, big hair, long legs, and a face like death—the woman's ready to walk the runway.

Where is her husband? Trying to squeeze all their jewels and gold coins and silk rugs in the trunk, no doubt. But the child is more important, the child must survive. Though judging by his screams, it's doubtful he'll last another hour.

I kneel down in front of the stroller. The baby smacks his lips together then swallows the spit. I'm sure it's the first time he's shut his mouth since last night. The front of his shirt is soaked through. His eyelashes are sticky and wet with tears. He reaches for me. I look up. Today anything could happen. Including getting smacked across the head with Mommy's purse. No, seems like she recognizes me. That night Elham got trashed and I made a scene, they were having a party. Back then she was still pregnant. And she was freaking out. She kept tugging at the back of her husband's shirt to get him to stay out of it. She's got to be, what, a good two decades younger than him. I unbuckle the seatbelt on the stroller. The baby opens and closes his fists and lifts his butt out of the seat, reaching. I can't take it anymore. Purse-smacking or not, it's worth it.

The child's mother looks at me in shock. Like I'm an angel sent from the skies especially for her. My lips get covered in spit. He's all over my face like a puppy. The mother gives me a grateful look. Her lips move up and down and—poof! she disappears. Fuck this MP3 player. I take my earbuds out. What did she say?

The woman sprints up the stairs two by two. The baby

grabs the cord and digs into my hair for the earbuds. I press the earbuds into his ears. He grabs one and stuffs it into his mouth.

His butt feels hot. Smells like shit. I try to put him in the stroller to see what state the diaper's in but he starts screaming again. I let it go, inspection passed.

"Nahid . . . Nahid!"

His dad's bald, bearded head pops out the window.

"I think your wife's gone upstairs!"

He frowns and the head disappears. Either the Mrs. needed to pee or she didn't want her husband sniffing out where she keeps her cash. Is she going to have to explain herself to her man during this fucking mess?

The baby's over it. He throws the earbuds in my face and leans his head against my chest. Would it have killed you to be a little more civilized?

Their Nissan Patrol sits in the middle of the courtyard with all four doors open. I take the stairs down to the basement apartment. I ring. Nothing. I bang the door knocker together. The baby grabs onto the bronze ring and tries to pull it toward his mouth.

I extract my phone from pocket #206 of my cargos and dial Parvin's home phone. The call goes through. I can hear the phone ringing through the door. It rings. And rings. And rings. No one picks up. Maybe Ashkan's not at home, maybe he's gone out.

I call Ashkan. *All circuits busy.* I call again. *All circuits busy*. The child pries the phone out of my hand and puts it in his mouth.

I take the chipped cement stairs two by two. Sounds

like a fight up on the second floor. Babe, your mother's secret is out—what do we do now? Or any clue where the Colonel might be? On the first floor, there's no sign of life behind the curtains. Does that mean the good sir's still asleep? I suppose we could act like grown-ups and ask him to let us in with the spare key . . . Nah, never mind. I'm in no mood to explain and grin and grovel and beg for help.

Shattering and breaking sounds get folded into the screams and shouts. The baby gives me a questioning look. Baba's yelling sounds familiar, huh? It's weird that the Colonel's gone MIA. And where's Crassus? Here, let's go try the side windows. Maybe Ashkan just dozed off. We can check for Crassus while we're over there. The bum's probably still asleep.

Crassus is lying in his usual spot in the rose bushes with his muzzle on his paws. When he sees us, he gets up and stretches nice and long. I crouch down and dig my fingers into the fur on his head. He yawns and gives himself a good shake, down to the last atom. The baby catches hold of Crassus's ear and pulls. Crassus rubs his nose against my knee still half-asleep. I put a hand under his muzzle and lift his head.

"You don't know where Ashkan is, do you?"

The child drops the phone and grabs one of Crassus's ears in each hand. They perk up at the sound of glass shattering. Crassus turns toward the noise.

"Don't worry about them. Do you know if Ashkan's home?"

I crouch down by the basement windows. You

can see the foot of the sofa through the curtains, but Ashkan's not on it. I rap on the window with my phone. I press my ear to the glass. Total silence. The kid's getting restless. He whimpers. Essence of shit paired with pee wafts from his behind. May you burn in hell, Ashkan.

I could try breaking the window to climb in and check things out. Maybe he's in Elham's room. I wish I hadn't taken you out of that damn stroller. Or I could try the deadbolt. Great, I'll just grab a screwdriver from your dad's toolbox right over there by his parking spot and we'll break in that way.

I stand on my tiptoes. I can't reach the deadbolt at the top. I set the baby on the steps. The screaming kicks off. I stand on my tiptoes again. The bolt's loose but I still can't reach high enough to get the screwdriver to engage. I stretch higher. The bolt clicks. I pick the baby up and give the door a shove. Repeat. I step back then charge. Crassus comes to help. All together we take a few steps back then one, two . . . three of us lie splattered on the living room floor.

The place is thick with fog. The bathroom door's ajar and I can hear the water running. Ashkan's in the corner wilting under the shower. He's slumped against the tiles, head drooped to one side. The water's coming down in daggers. His hair falls forward over his face. I press the light switch. It doesn't work. Nothing ever works around here. I push his hair out of his face.

Pale as ash. The baby starts shrieking. It's dark and stinks of Parvin; he's not into it. I take Ashkan's pulse. I can't feel anything under my fingers. I try his neck.

There I sense some warmth and movement but can't tell if it's coming from Ashkan's neck or my own fingers. By now the baby's screaming so loudly my eardrums are about to burst. God, what made me take you out of that stroller?

I take the baby back to the living room and set him on the floor. He looks around like he doesn't know what hit him. Crassus is sprawled out on the sofa with his head nestled in the pillows. He yawns. Rescued from the dark fog, the kid's eyes fill with gratitude—but as soon as he realizes that I'm going back in and he's staying put, he starts screaming again.

I take Ashkan by the armpits and drag him out. Boy, you're pretty damn heavy for a bag of bones. Fuck me. If I'd only set out a little earlier, I would've found you on the couch, phone in hand, crying and chain smoking. When did you send that last message? If only I'd texted you something nice and soothing before heading out. I should've told Bobak. Bobak would know just what to say to calm you down—the same shit he uses to ruin all of Maman's arias right before the climax, presumably—and then I wouldn't be over here right now sweating like a donkey. I drag Ashkan into the living room. Now the baby's cries sound more like a beggar's drunk lament. He shuts his mouth for a second and gives me a teary, skeptical look. He can't work it out: Should he act happy to see me, or does this fickle lover just make him want to scream? That won't help your case, my sweet. You freak out and it only makes me more likely to leave. He ponders the issue. That's right, give it a good think.

Try to act reasonably. High expectations, I know, but do your best. It's like he hears me. Who knows, maybe we just pulled off telepathy.

I take Ashkan by the armpits again and drag him over to the sofa. His clothes smell musty. How long were you in there, crazy? I turn his face to one side. He coughs and the spit lands on my face. Crassus lifts his mug and peers at Ashkan through droopy eyelids.

I tilt him in the direction he's leaning to lay his head down sideways. But what if he vomits and his throat locks up? I take the cushion off the sofa, lift his torso, and drop him onto the cushion stomach down.

Per usual the fridge smells like mold. I take out the milk. How many years ago did it expire? The child's mother materializes like a smoking genie.

Her eyes latch on to Ashkan's inert body. Evidently the child prefers to ignore his mother. The tapes and CDs strewn on the floor are keeping him busy.

"Is something wrong?" she asks.

"No, his blood pressure must have dropped in the shower so he fainted. That's all."

"Do you want me to have my husband—?"

Midsentence she changes her mind. I know what she's thinking, I can tell from the way her mouth hangs open and her eyes dart back and forth. She's thinking about how this whole family's a pain in the ass. How once every couple of months, shit hits the fan and it's one of these idiots who took the dump. Parvin gets drunk and reminisces about her days in the struggle then sets everyone marching through the courtyard singing the Labor Party anthem, or Elham comes home trashed and ruins their party by getting in a fight with the cabbie, or Ashkan tries killing himself and drops a cigarette that ends up setting the carpet on fire.

I need to get rid of her. I pick up the child. He looks at me wide-eyed but before he can figure out what's going on, I push him into his mother's arms. Now he looks at me like I've royally fucked him over and he starts screaming. Guess the apathy's mutual—I have to press the kid into his mother's chest three or four times and hard before his mother finally takes him.

"My husband—do you want me to . . . I . . ."

"No no, a spoonful of sugar will sort him out."

With that I paint a big, wide grin on my face that says everything's just as it should be. She backs out of the room. The child's cries bounce off the walls in the garage and echo in my ears. Fuck me. I shut the door. The sound plays back in reverse.

I take Ashkan and turn him over. Listen up, my friend—fixing up lovesick fools like you is my specialty but today there isn't a single hospital with space for us to go get your stomach pumped. Please, Ashkan, on your ancestors' souls I'm begging you: drink this milk and try to chuck.

I guess he can hear me. His lips part and he takes a sip. Sips two and three I funnel down his throat before he knows what's hit him. His eyelids flip open and slowly lower back down. I pour more milk down his throat. He opens his eyes and looks at me like he doesn't recognize me.

I hold his head back to pour more milk down the tube. He closes his eyes. Milk streams out of the corner of his mouth.

"Please, Ashkan. Pretty please. Swallow."

I turn his head to the side and slap him in the face.

"Ashkan, open your eyes. Ashkan, look at me."

He opens his eyes. Tears bubble up and boil over, and by now his stomach must be boiling too. He props himself up on his elbows, his shoulders lift up, and the milk goes flying. Okay, repeat and—bingo! A few black specks hit the wall. I am one lucky motherfucker. Looks like you took the opium with cold water and your stomach acids weren't strong enough to break it down. Either that or you swallowed the whole twenty-five grams and now this speck or two is all you're willing to spare. I fish through his fluids for the leftovers.

"Why won't you people leave me alone?" he groans.

I sniff at the pieces.

"Hey, when did you get hold of this shit?"

"Can't you just leave me alone?"

"I know this stuff isn't Parvin's."

"Just fuck off, will you?"

Now that he's yelled he starts blubbering. I lean against the wall, rest his head on my lap, and comb my fingers through his hair. He digs his face into my stomach and sobs.

"Leave me alone."

I push his hair back from over his forehead, I comb his eyebrows with the tips of my fingers, I swipe the wet under his eyes across his cheeks. He sobs.

"Leave me alone."

His shoulders swing up again and his stomach boils over. A yellow goo spills out onto the carpet and he starts coughing. I rub his shoulders. He heaves. He cries. He heaves . . . He cries . . . He heaves. A yellow goo spills out.

"Mrs. Yazdanbakhsh? Mrs. Yazdanbakhsh!"

The Colonel's raspy voice drills into my skull, suspended above the *click-clack* of his cane like the dominant note in a sonata.

"Mrs. Yazdanbakhsh? Mrs. Parvin! Miss Elham! Mr. Ashkan!"

He keeps on shouting.

"What's going on down there? Miss Elham? Mrs. Karamati is up here saying that Mr. Yazdanbakhsh's tried killing himself again. Mr. Yazdanbakhsh!"

Fuck. It's my own damn fault for plucking that pup of hers out of the stroller. Okay, forza. Today I will not be afraid of the Colonel. No, screw that. Today I feel like messing with the Colonel. I'll open the door and say, *Yes, Colonel, sir!* Unfortunately Mr. Yazdanbakhsh has indeed tried to kill himself, but see how's he's been a good boy? In order to not set fire to the carpeting and to stop you from making a scene, he went and had his cigarette in the shower so that even if he dropped it, it wouldn't burn the house down. Now, if you please, fuck off.

"Mrs. Yazdanbakhsh! Is anybody in there? Why won't you open the door? Mr. Yazdanbakhsh?"

I can't *not* open the door—he's about to break it off the hinges . . . The *click-clack* of his cane echoes in the courtyard. He must be trying to peer through the windows. Don't waste your energy. You can't really see much of the sofa, and you definitely won't be able see Ashkan and me sitting next to it on the floor. And I'm not opening that damn door.

"Mrs. Yazdanbakhsh? Mr. Ashkan!"

Crassus is sprawled out on the sofa like he couldn't care less, like me. So you're not afraid of the Colonel anymore either?

"Miss Elham! Ms. Yazdanbakhsh!"

The old man's got that bad back of his creased so neatly that his nose is down by his slippers as he raps a carnelian signet ring against the glass. Crassus closes his eyes and yawns.

"Mrs. Yazdanbakhsh!"

Now he's over by the kitchen window. He's bent over, rapping on the glass. You can stand there hollering till the roosters crow and I'm still not opening that goddamn door. But please, sir, do be careful not to break your back. Crassus sits up and perks his ears. What's wrong, boy?

The ground slips out from under my ass. The sofa sways back and forth. Crassus barks. Ashkan's head rolls onto the floor. The windows jingle and jangle. The Colonel's cane—no! Shards of glass fly into my face and the old man's head falls through the window.

The Colonel's head falls through the basement window but his shriveled-up shoulders get stuck in the window frame. Crassus looks at me wide-eyed, ears perked.

"Let's go check it out."

Crassus runs up the stairs two by two. The Colonel's lying facedown in his white jersey pajamas and kaftan robe. The prehistoric slippers are still on his feet. Crassus circles him, reluctant to get too close.

"Colonel? Sir?"

I feel like my own voice is coming from somewhere far far away. I don't know what or where to touch. Crassus circles the body over and over again while issuing something like a whimper. I pull the Colonel's arm out of the kaftan. Damn that's cold. I should take his pulse.

His carnelian ring knocks around his spindly finger. It feels like a bunch of bones wrapped in paper. Touching his skin sends a shiver up my spine. I let go. What's the point anyway? Pulse or no pulse, what difference?

Suppose he has a pulse, as in he's alive. Then what, I run outside and scream for help so someone comes to save him? What moron is going to go out of their way to save a dinosaur like this? The man's the same age as Dear Uncle himself. Move over *My Uncle Napoleon*, there's a new guy in town.

Maybe some such moron does in fact exist. But me, I don't have the energy for all that yelling and screaming. I'm not cut out for that type of work. How am I supposed to explain what this bitch's head is doing hanging through the window? Crassus is back in his usual spot stretched out in the rose bushes; seems like we're on the same page. According to dog logic he must've figured that the Colonel's either watching TV or working on his tan. The old man's bony, hairless legs stick out of his pant cuffs. His cracked heels look like Mesozoic fossils. Lord, what will I do with the body?

I need to think. I need to activate that gray matter and think like Poirot. I need a smoke.

I run down the steps two by two. Crassus beats me there and claims the sofa. I pull out a pack of cigarettes from pocket #207 of my cargos and lie on the floor next to Ashkan. He's tipped way over and his pretty, plump lips are open just a crack. Dammit, my lighter's missing. Newton's Second Law: thou shalt keep thy lighter within a half-meter radius at all times. Then there's the Third Law . . . And the Fourth . . . I put the cigarette between my lips and go through the roster. I can't get up. A gurgle of some sort comes out of Ashkan's mouth. My god. What a fucking sound—how much did you take?

Crassus materializes with a lighter between his teeth.

"You're a dream."

He nuzzles his snout into my neck and plops his stinky ass down on my chest.

"Enough. Get up, you slut."

I inhale and swish the smoke around my mouth. My jaw muscles warm up. I inhale again and push the smoke down deep into my chest. The veins in my neck relax. I close my eyes. I inhale again and pull the smoke up through my nose. The blood vessels in my forehead relax. I inhale. And inhale. And inhale. Any second now and the gray matter will start doing its thing. Then I'll be able to think. Figure out what to do with the bodies . . . Figure out . . .

I open my eyes. The Colonel stares back at me like a buck head mounted on the wall. An abstract painting, blood streams from the old man's throat down onto Parvin's Che Guevara poster and over the star on Che's forehead, where it gets lost in the black shadows on his face to reemerge out of Che's left nostril.

The Colonel's thick, red blood streams out Che's nose freakishly fast into a palm-sized pool of blood on the carpet. Oh Parvin, if only you were here to offer a few lines in honor of this epic neighbor of yours. Who knows, half of Tehran's probably already dead due to such innocent circumstances as the slip of a cane while spying on one's tenants.

So Arash was right after all—all the assholes are either dying off or making a break for it. Fuck you all for leaving me alone with Ashkan on a day like this. Where the hell is everyone?

Elham's hot-pink bathrobe flares behind the open door. When did she head out? Didn't she know Ashkan wasn't feeling well? Who was it this time? What difference does it make.

I hit the light switch. The LED's white light and Elham's Versace perfume swirl through my skull. The bed's unmade, still stamped with the outline of her body. Like her round ass and arched back just got up off the plush mattress. I feel like lying in her bed.

My hard, bony butt knocks around the shapely crater. I turn on my side and stuff my face into the pillow. Wafts of shampoo and conditioner and lotion and a thousand other bullshit products stream into my skull. Who would've thought a person could craft herself into such a pretty peach in this cave, in this hole, in this dank, sunless cellar of the dear Colonel's that you've managed to lighten up through the strident efforts of halogen bulbs—how *do* you do it, Elham? And why aren't you here now? Why aren't you here to take Ashkan in your arms and shower him with kisses like you always do after the two of you fight to the death? I shut my eyes. The towel's still damp. What about them? Ashkan, Parvin? You can't just abandon them on a day like today.

And why can't you? When will you stop dealing with their crazy? I mean, why should we give a fuck if our mothers were classmates then comrades back in the day? Now that my Maman Minoo's on the road to Kelardasht with her darling Bobak towing a suitcase full of evening gowns so she can sit around the poker table on the porch with a valley view, bleeding some rich suckers dry, and your Maman Parvin's out there combing the streets for the final survivors from her activist days, what is it to you or me if Azar's lying six feet under, who knows where? Why do you and me and Sara have to be heirs to all this insanity?

A dose of dog breath sprays me in the face.

"Crassus!"

I dig my fingers into his fur. He looks at me sadly.

"Don't give me that look . . . Please?"

He puts his paws on the pillow, rests his muzzle on top, and stares straight into my eyes.

"Do you know how pretty your eyes are? Something's wrong with them. Leaving you here, who does that?"

You lift your head and gaze at me languidly. As if to say, *Yeah, I know.*

You yawn and your tongue sticks out. I stick my hand in your mouth. Now you're pissed at me for messing up your yawn. You bite down softly and howl. Go ahead, whine. That night I went too hard, you sat beside me the morning after just like this, howling each time I moaned. And when the ice pack had melted on my blazing forehead, you took it to the kitchen for a refill and came back with Elham, who stood over the two of us with her hands on her hips then burst out laughing.

Come and let's howl together again. But my darling

dumbass, know that today, no matter how much we might bark or yelp, nobody else is coming. Not even Elham for the sake of a laugh. Maybe she's finally found her Prince Charming, the one who was supposed to arrive on a white stallion and . . .

Hell, given her commitment to the search, it's entirely possible. Examining all the guys with good hair who slam the brakes on their Beamers or zero out their Xantias to pull up next to her.

Look at that, Crassus—Elham hasn't taken any of her favorite things. All her tanks and jeans and manteaus and coats and décolleté dresses are hanging nice and neat from the hooks on the wall. Which means she can't have left for good! Which means she hasn't tracked down Prince Charming.

Maybe the door's about to swing open and Elham will walk in with Ali or Siavash or Behzad holding a bottle of something and throwing her infectious laughter into the air. Which will wake up Ashkan, who'll rub his eyes and wash his face and take a seat on the sofa next to Ali or Siavash or Behzad or Amir or Shahryar or Kiarash or Kourush or Saman so they can raise a glass and drink to the Colonel's demise.

I hit Play on the stereo. A sample from an old Dashti song gets lost in the blues melody of an electric guitar. Dear god, Elham listens to this shit? I press Stop. You open your eyes and whimper. Sorry! Don't tell me that's what you use to warm up. So when Elham sits in front of the mirror in the mornings dolling herself up, you take the opportunity to train your howl. Okay, okay. Practice makes perfect, maybe you'll eventually master a vibrato as good as this poor soul's.

"The beloved's reflection shiiiees from me and my heart sighs

"My pleasure is eternal aaahh!

"My pleasure is eternal with the red of desire . . . ooohh!"

I grab a hair extension teeming with rhinestones and fake gems and put it on my head. Tell me, Elham, is your pleasure truly eternal? With those rich kids and their Land Cruisers and their plastic noses, who on their best behavior barely think to turn to you in bed and ask, *You good?* Well, Elham, are you?

Yeah, you're good. Go ahead, breathe those fake moans and groans in their ears, "Ich komme, ich komme."

"O rebellious fortune, hold me tight

"First sip from the golden chalice, next—"

Yes? Do tell. What's next and when will it ever arrive? Crassus, what do you think? So many tubes and tweezers and clippers and bottles and brushes. A never-ending war against excess hair growth. The only thing that's not considered excess is the hair on your head, did you know that, Crassus? But then what's the rest for? The epilator's already plugged in, ready to eradicate the smallest sprout of hair from the earth's surface as soon as it rears its ugly head. I turn it on. The gears start turning. The metal prongs close in and grip the hairs and—ow!

A tub of cold wax, a pile of Veet strips. Final touches require tweezers. Elham's taking her pinchers to the grave, as Parvin likes to say.

"We don't know much about clerics or clergy,

"Just give us the chalice or a story."

Yeah, that's it, a story. Ashkan's always saying the same thing. Story, please!

There's some dramatic humming followed by:

"The beloved's reflection shiiiees from me and my heart sighs

"My pleasure is eternal aahh."

The ring of the telephone echoes in my skull. Maybe it's Parvin. Or Elham. Maybe they're stuck somewhere and they're trying to check up on Ashkan.

"Allo, yes?"

"Elham?"

The nasally whine of a thick-necked, flabby-ass creature travels over the line.

"Elham, is that you?"

His voice quivers.

"Elham?"

I stay quiet.

"Is that you, Elham?"

Silence.

"Elham, please, I—" he chokes out.

A series of suppressed sobs. He's definitely one of them—good hair, decent nose job—and Elham's stomped on his heart with both feet. I sigh and slowly release the smoke from my cigarette. This way he'll think it's really her. Elham does it all the time, lets them talk their hearts out while giving the silent treatment. Lets them yell and scream and curse.

"Elham, I'm sorry. I know I—god! What happened?"

What happened indeed. He sucks in his snot, sobs, sucks in his snot again.

"Elham, I swear I had no idea. I just—dear god!"

Listening to rich assholes whine about their nonexistent problems really takes it out of you. I hang up.

The phone rings. And rings. And rings.

"Elham, please don't hang up. I'm begging you."

I hang up.

It rings and rings and rings and rings.

Crassus opens his eyes a sliver and grumbles.

"Fine, you win."

I pick up.

"Elham, I swear I don't know those people. I've never seen them before in my life."

His voice sounds normal again. Must have cleared out the snot supply with the tears. I spot an empty Pam Pam cake wrapper by the remote. Guess Ashkan figured he'd wreck his gut if he threw back all that opium on an empty stomach.

"God, seriously! Elham, I'm begging you, listen to me. I—well I—I mean, it's just that—"

He's sobbing again. I hit Play on the DVD player. The *whir* of a Super 8 camera accompanies a shot of Parvin in her youth, laughing soundlessly. She takes an impish, curly haired baby Elham into her arms and holds the baby's fingers up to the camera. Elham flails around and manages to escape. More sobbing and snot sucking and—Crassus jumps onto the sofa and licks my neck. So this is one of your domestic rituals, leaping into Ashkan's lap when the Super 8 hums? How many times a day does the sap watch this trash?

The sobbing cuts off. It's completely quiet. He's probably clearing out the tank with his hand over the mouthpiece. He takes a deep breath. Wonderful. The guy's gathering his strength for some real talk.

"Elham, I can't even remember—what I mean is, I was super far gone last night. I—I think . . . that's never happened to me before!"

The last line comes out as a shout so he starts crying again. What the fuck did you do last night to solicit such tears? Crassus barks. Sheesh, I know, I know. I'm supposed to announce each cast member as they make an appearance, just like Ashkan does. I rewind by a few seconds. Look, see that hand entering the frame to hand Parvin a kabob skewer? That's my father. Evidently they had kabobs way back then too. And that girl with the ponytail, that's my mother. No really! Stop groaning, she looks a little different, that's all. The sobbing's cut off again and now he's blowing his nose. What's left to eject, his brains? I rewind. Baba's arm takes the kabob out of Parvin's hand and draws back out of the frame, Bobak walks backward and gives me my doll. I wail. My mouth stretches big as a saucer. Crassus grumbles. What, you're not into watching the video in reverse? But it's more fun this way. It's not? Okay, okay.

"Elham . . . I can't even remember—I don't know whether—god!"

If you can't remember how you even fucked up, what's with all the whining?

Check it out, Crassus. See that couple with their arms around each other all lovey-dovey? That's Sara's parents. Stop licking my ear, there's no need to thank me. And that guy with furrowed eyebrows who's fanning the coals under the kabobs and shaking his head as he hums a folk song—that's Ashkan's dad. Yeah I get it, don't start with me. I know I'm supposed to pause on the close-up of his thick mustache and white teeth and smiling eyes.

Sigh. Doesn't seem so bad, does it, a few frames of some guy fanning kabobs being the only image you have of your father.

"Elham, please say something. Anything. Well, maybe not *anything* . . ."

I hang up.

"Hey, Crassus, want to come back to our place? If Maman and Bobak are finally gone, we can chill on the couch and watch TV and smoke while we wait for Nana Molouk to get home. How does that sound?"

You rub your nose on mine.

"Attaboy, you're great. Let me just make a phone call to see if these suckers are on the road yet."

Maman picks up on the first ring.

"Allo? Allo?"

Then she starts yelling outside the receiver: "Bobak! Bobak, come here, it's Shadi, I just know. Bobak! *It's Shadi.* Come talk to her. Bobak!"

There's sound of Bobak hurdling over sofas and tables and chairs.

"Shadi! Please don't hang up."

How do they know it's me?

"Shadi, Baba will be here in ten minutes. Quit fooling around and come home."

Ten minutes? Have you looked outside? This dipshit thinks he's in Paris.

"Shadi, please."

It's completely quiet. Not even Miss Gelin makes a peep. Maybe Arash actually put her on the back of his bike and let her go in Mohseni Square. Or maybe they're all holding their breath waiting for me to say something. What fucking idiots. Why don't they just go?

"Shadi."

Crassus lifts his head and barks into the phone.

"So you're at Elham's?"

Nice, Crassus, now they know where we are.

"Shadi, hand Elham the phone. Shadi."

Bobak whispers my name like he's invoking some ancient goddess. I like it. Makes me feel good. I put a cigarette in my mouth and search my pockets. Dammit, I'm always breaking the Second Law. Crassus runs to the other room and comes back with a lighter between his teeth. A different one. A red barbecue lighter. Buddy, have you got a stash of lighters hiding somewhere? Now tell the truth.

"Shadi, look, you're not supposed to be alone. I mean—what I meant was . . ."

Maman's sobbing starts up again. I click the barbecue lighter on. I inhale and hold the smoke on my tongue.

"Shadi."

He whimpers. How many different ways can you say my name? And how many has he managed since breakfast? I inhale and draw the smoke up through my nose.

"Shadi. Please."

I want to tell you that Ashkan's lying at my feet on the floor heaving. I want to tell you that the Colonel's head is hanging through the window like a stuffed deer. I want to tell you that . . . I inhale and swallow the smoke.

As soon as I hit the main drag, two kids with Afros slam into me on rollerblades then get lost in the crowd. A slew of boys and birdlike girls are pouring out of Darband Street. The leader of the group walks backward pumping both fists overhead. All of them look pissed and they're yelling at the top of their lungs. Some kid with a phone to his ear whispers something to the leader. The leader jumps onto the roof of a Peugeot and sticks his fists up again. Everyone holds their breath. What will he say?

"Listen up, my friends—they've just surrendered Narmak Square. This city is ours!"

They yell and cheer and whistle and scream with all they've got. The boys lift the birds onto their shoulders. The birds stretch their arms overhead and take a breath: "Whose city our city, and you can't take it back! Whose city our city, and we're here to paint it black!"

A couple gays hop in front and start shaking their hips like belly dancers. The birds coil around them. Is this for real? These people make Arash look sane. I have half a mind to get in there myself and show them what's what. Tajrish Square is lined bumper-to-bumper with a fleet of riot police Benzes and there are two helicopters parked on the grass. Guess they expect the next earthquake to come from the sky. I feel a hand brush my back. I turn around.

"My sincere apologies."

It's one of the kids on rollerblades. He stretches his maw into a jackal-jawed grin. Braces and crooked teeth. Who the fuck? He winks and disappears into the crowd. Another hand brushes my back.

"My sincere apologies."

Same kid. He stretches his maw. Sparkling straight white teeth. Must be his twin brother.

"My sincere apologies."

I turn around and it's Thing One. Now they're both standing there staring at me with maws stretched into jackal-jawed grins. One swipes my backpack and melts into the crowd. The other zooms in the opposite direction. Thing One tosses my backpack to Thing Two. Who do I go after? The earth slips out from under my feet. Screams rush into my ears. The birds somersault off the boys' shoulders. Bodies pile onto one another. Arms and legs drop by to say hi. The birds giggle and shriek. The boys hoot and holler . . . I stretch out on the grass. Put my ear to the ground. I don't want to have to listen to them. I don't want to. All the screaming and shouting and yelling and laughing is making me sick. Can't you idiots shut the fuck up? Shut up for just one second. And listen! Listen to the earth's tremors. To everything moving down there. To all the stuff that came loose last night that's clacking and clanging. Listen. If you'd stop screaming for a single second, you'd hear it. Put your ear to the ground like me and listen. Listen. The streets are speaking. I can hear the pavement cracking. Snapping and sputtering, cracking its knuckles after a long day. It's tired. Tired. Tired. Listen, you assholes.

Thing One and Thing Two are leaning over me. The kid with braces holds out my backpack.

"Sorry."

That comes from the one with nice teeth. He's got his hands in his pockets and his head hangs low. I take the backpack. My stomach turns. I don't know what it is about two people looking exactly the same, but twins gross me out. They disappear back into the crowd. Like cartoon roaches, riot cops skitter out of who knows where, gas masks on, shields out. They surround the square. The chief keeps a steady stream going into his walkie-talkie. Must have used a numbing spray on his face—not a single muscle moves when he talks.

Now the birds are rushing back and forth yelling, "Charge!" and scraping their bodies against the soldier's shields. "Charge!" Back and forth. But now the birds stand back. A pair of arms and legs gets dragged on the ground. A mouth opens. Shouts. Familiar shouts . . . Screaming . . . Screaming . . . I push my way through the crowd and—her long white hair drags on the ground. What the fuck are *you* doing here?

Camo fatigues. Borrowed big boots. She shouts. Kicks and screams at the cops crowded around her. What are you doing here? And what are you wearing? And why is your hair dragging on the ground? Please stop kicking them . . . She shouts then disappears into the background, into a sea of black cars.

"Nana Molouk?"

I start pushing through the Green Suits elbows out. A wall of chests blocks my way. That's my grandmother! I stand on my tiptoes. Where are you taking her?

"That's my grandmother . . ."

My shouts fade away. Her shouts fade away . . . She runs toward me. She's escaped! A blow to the back of the knees and she folds. Her long white hair drags on the ground.

I need to break through the police line. I need to tell them that she's my grandmother, she has Alzheimer's, she—up swings the baton . . . My jaw burns . . . Pain shoots down my sides. I shield my head with my hands. Pain shoots up my arms. Go go go. The wall of flesh pushes me back. I get lost in a mess of limbs. The pain travels down my neck, unfurls through my body. The crowd sways back and forth like jello, sways back and forth, goes black.

"Did she open her eyes yet?"

My ears are ringing. My lips taste like salt.

"Those bastards really fucked her up."

I try to sit up and pain shoots up my arms. Something's on fire in my chest. I can't breathe.

"Girl, you've got as much sparkle right now as flat Fanta."

Four or five faces come and go. Where am I? I feel dizzy, I can't see.

"We were just standing there when—"

I can't breathe. I swallow the saltiness.

"Does it hurt?"

I try hard to pry my jaw apart.

"Like hell."

"Was that actually your grandma?"

I open my eyes. Some kid with a crooked nose smiles down at me. I exhale. The light hurts my eyes.

"Yeah."

"That's so cool."

My head spins. I shut my eyes. What's going on? Nana Molouk in camo. Where am I? And where did they take her? I have to go find her. What was she doing in that outfit? I need to get up. I need to go find her.

"Where did they take her?" I ask.

"Don't worry, they won't do anything to her, just lock her up."

That comes from a kid with his hair shaved into diamonds like a pineapple. He's smirking in my face. I take my beanie off. The pain's making me sweat.

"Let me make sure you haven't broken a rib or something."

A pudgy girl with kind eyes slides her fingers along my body. I shut my eyes and hold my breath.

"Relax, she's practically a doctor. Just give it another seven or eight years."

Who said that? How many of them are there? The soft, chubby fingers walk up my ribs, up, up—fuck, I can't breathe.

"Just breathe."

"Ayy!"

"Nothing's broken but you might have a fracture."

Thanks, genius. I open my eyes. The chubby girl's gone. Instead a boy's zitty face stares down at me looking worried.

"Those bastards really know how to fuck a person up. Out by Tandis Mall they've crippled a few folks. On orders—word on the street is the prisons are full."

That's coming from another kid with an Afro. Where am I? Who are these people? Why are there so many of them? The heads bob up and down and the light makes my eyes sting. I shut my eyes.

"Where are they locking them up?"

"Who knows, wherever they can."

Some kid who looks like bin Laden bends over me.

"But which prison?"

"Nobody knows. Don't worry about it. This city is ours now. Your grandma gets through the night and she's golden."

"Word is Resalat's ours now too."

An itsy-bitsy bird leaning against the wall says that then holds a barbecue lighter up to her cigarette. I close my eyes.

"We should head to Vanak. We're wasting time."

I open my eyes. Now there's some rangy stick girl leaning against the wall where the bird used to be. What the hell is going on? And what's with this switcheroo trick? Was I hit in the head?

"So what are we going to do about Shemiran?"

Some guy with a beard takes the cigarette from stick girl—wait, it's not the same girl. This one's a beach blond wearing a school-uniform hijab. The other one had olive tones. I'm going insane.

"Where am I?"

"Sadaf Mall."

The steel gate rolls up. Four or five people walk in, two or three walk out. Some beefy buzzcut with tatted-up biceps a half meter in girth strolls in leading a pack of five or six of his decals.

"Everybody relax. This city is ours."

Arash's dumb-ass logic is spreading like a breed of Barbapapa. Was the earth fractured or just these idiots' skulls? *This city is ours*—I'd really like to know what that actually means.

I need to get out of this damn lunatic asylum and fast. I sit up and put my beanie back on. The chubby girl smiles.

"Don't make yourself dizzy!"

But why does she look different now? The last doctor lady didn't have all that hair on her chin. I need to get out of here. I stand up, it makes me dizzy. I reach down for the bench.

"Don't get up."

Some curly haired guy with a mustache fit for

Genghis Khan comes up to me. I shut my eyes and take a deep breath.

"I'm fine."

"Where are you trying to go? I'll give you ride."

I smile.

"In this gridlock? Does your car fly?"

"Girl, who said anything about a car?"

This line's delivered by a pretty ponytail leaning against a gorgeous green Kawasaki KMX. Now this one's something else. I'll go to the ends of the earth with this one.

A few friendly pats on the back.

"Be well."

"Take care."

"We're headed to Vanak."

"See you there?"

The gate rolls up and Tattoos walks out with his ten or twenty mini-mes. I shut my eyes. I suppose Ponytail's vanished only to be replaced by some bald and curly clown on an electric bike.

Ponytail laughs in my face.

"So what's the deal, you some sort of crisscrosser or something?"

Look who's talking.

"Think of me as an older sister, my friend."

"Well, then what's with the hat?"

"Just for the hell of it."

"Can't be just that."

He's got this "fuck it" way of talking that clashes with his clean look, and that smirk creeping on his lips isn't going anywhere. He takes a tony pipe out of his pocket and lights it.

"So where do you want to go?"

Where *do* I want to go? Where did Nana Molouk get that getup? And why does she have to look like that on a day like today? My legs give out. I sit down on the bench and take my head in my hands. Maybe if I get the blood flowing I can think.

"Where do they take the people they round up?"

"Why, want to go?"

"Can you?"

"Are you okay?"

I lift my head and stare at his pretty oaken hair.

"No."

He laughs and flaunts a row of white teeth. A flash of gold at the corner of his lips glints then passes out of sight.

"Gold tooth?"

"Gold? Girl, you must be dreaming."

He scowls then cracks up.

"You still haven't said where you want to go."

He fixes me with his kind eyes. Let me think. Don't look at me like that. Don't look at me. I shut my eyes and put my head in my hands. Nana Molouk. Ashkan. Just one hit. Siamak. Where's Rahim? Sara's waiting. Someone is surrendering the soul. Where did they take Nana Molouk? What the fuck is wrong with her? In that outfit? Out of a million and one ways to go insane, why did she have to choose that one?

"You worried about your granny?"

I must not open my eyes. I must not open my eyes. Must not. Must not. Must not.

"Don't worry, they won't do anything to her."

I open my eyes. I can think better this way.

"I promise she's okay. But so . . . she's gone off a little, right?"

"Yeah."

"Same thing happened to mine."

He blows smoke out of his nose.

"She died."

The smell of Captain Black tobacco swirls through my skull. My skin tickles like crazy, like he aimed the smoke straight at me.

"Shit, what did they do to your face!"

Now he's squatting down in front of me with the pipe hanging out of the side of his mouth. He looks at me good and hard. I get up. Pain swirls through my chest.

"Can you take me up to Darakeh?"

"At your service. But it'll cost you a clean twenty thousand tomans."

My skin's still chirping.

"I don't get you. The pieces don't fit?"

He gives a little laugh and slips his pipe into his jacket pocket.

"What doesn't fit what, sister?"

I cock my head to one side and take a good look at him.

"Can't tell if you're uptown or downtown! You're like some kind of collage."

The little laugh stretches a little longer.

"A collage! That's good, I'll give you that."

He hops on the bike and nods at me to get on.

"I wouldn't have pegged you for a cabbie."

"A cabbie, come on? I just feel like giving you a lift."

I hop on the bike and cling on to his jacket. The pain starts from under my ribs and travels up through my neck.

"Then what's with the clean twenty thou?"

"Consider it a donation."

He turns around to stretch his maw into a jackal-jawed grin and the gold at the corner of his mouth gleams. The steel door rolls up. Ponytail weaves his Komex through people and cars on the street and sidewalk.

"Took you for one of those crisscrossers at first."

"How do you know I'm not?"

"You're just not, don't mess with me. It's not the same style."

He turns and smiles over his shoulder. I smile back.

"Sounds like you know what you're talking about."

"You know."

He turns onto the first side street and zigzags through the cars. I clasp on to his jacket. Genuine leather. A bitter smell sinks into my chest. Is it the jacket or the ponytail?

He stands up. The tight one-way is packed bumper-to-bumper with two rows of cars. There's a family who's got their Pajero parked halfway out the gates and they're loading the car right there in the middle of the street. Meanwhile ten cars are coming at us going the wrong way. Even if the Pajero pulls in, and it most certainly won't, it'll take hours to untangle this mess. Ponytail rides onto the sidewalk. A few meters ahead, the sidewalk's been commandeered by a private garden as lush with roses and African violets as a miniature painting.

"Hell's bells, what have we here . . . Babe, do me a favor and hop off for a second."

He gets off himself then lifts the bike and passes it over the chain.

"Hey, you! What do you think you're doing?"

An old man starched to the nines waves his cane at Ponytail, shouting with all the breath he has left in him. The veins on his neck stick out thick as sewage pipes.

"Can't you see someone planted these flowers! Can't you see the chain?"

"No, man, I can't."

Ponytail hops onto the bike, and I hop on behind.

"No manners, no integrity, were you raised by wolves?"

He looks at me over his shoulder. Another smirk settles in his eyes.

"Should I make him pay?"

"He's an old man," I say. "Let it go."

"Come on, let me make him pay."

Ponytail laughs and mischief shoots from his eyes. He hits the kickstand and climbs off nice and slow. He saunters over to the old man and stops to stand in front of him with his hands on his hips. He looks back at me and winks.

"Look, bro, as far as I can tell you're getting the fuck out of here, but on your way out you're taking a shit all over the street. So what the fuck is it to you what *I* get up to? It's my city, brother, and I feel like stepping on the flowers. I feel like knocking shit down. Maybe I even feel like taking a piss. Does that upset you? Then stand up and protect your city! You man enough for that?"

The old man doesn't budge. He's stares into Ponytail's eyes uncomprehendingly. I feel bad for him. The way he looks at him, it's not angry and it's not afraid. He simply can't compute, can't comprehend what this mass of flesh and bones standing there, hands on his hips, puffing his chest, could possibly be saying.

"Stand up if you've got the balls. Stand up and make sure no one's left any stains on your pretty little town."

Ponytail spits the pulp from the match he's been chewing on at the old man's feet. Suddenly a sprightly little old woman flies out the front door, takes the old man by the arm, and pulls. His feet drag on the cobblestone and the *click-clack* of his cane rings in my ears. I shut my eyes. Where is Nana Molouk? The baton swings up and white hair drags on the pavement.

"Hey, you okay?"

Ponytail is right there in front of me. The fire in his eyes has gone out. It's been replaced by worry, plus something else I can't figure out. The old man turns to take a last look at us. The old woman pulls on his arm.

"You coming?"

I hop on the back of the bike and clasp on to his jacket. He zigzags through alleys and backstreets. Weaves through cars. I close my eyes. It doesn't smell like leather anymore and his hair's stopped dancing on my skin. Against my eyelids the trees cast shadows that come and go. I wonder what Sara and Siamak are doing right now. Bet they don't even know there was an earthquake. Siamak's lying there finishing off a hookah, head on Sara's lap, drags worthy of a Safavid king. I want to go to sleep. Rest my head on Ponytail's cold leather shoulder and sleep.

The wet cool of the trees settles on my cheeks. A whiff of Darakeh swirls through my skull. Any second now I'll get all nostalgic and reminisce about my buddies from college. From the dorm . . . The room in Darakeh. Chilling. Rahim. Majid. Rolling the wick. Tinfoil. Just three hits. Three hits and you're hitting the clouds. Falling in the river. Lying on the gravel. Three more hits. Just three. Now you're walking with your eyes closed. Chilling. Rahim. Majid . . . Oh fuck me.

It smells like smoke, like an overheating engine. That's not what Darakeh smells like—I open my eyes. A thousand cars and creatures and monsters and motorcycles are all tangled up in a knot. Ponytail slides the match to the other side of his mouth and cuts the engine.

"Look at all these fuckers!"

He glances at me over his shoulder. I'm waiting for the follow-up: *Sorry, sister, road's closed.* I frown.

"I think I'll get there faster if I walk."

"Do you really have to go?"

"My friend isn't doing so well—I'm scared of what he might do to himself if I'm too late."

Sorry, Ashkan. I just don't have it in me to walk all the way to Sara's.

"Where exactly are you trying to go?"

"Khoddami Street, by the park."

I chew on my lip. I need to put more feeling into it. I need to actually think about Ashkan. Move the clock back by a few hours to imagine Ashkan sitting there like he was, fully dressed in the shower with water beating down on his head. Or no, the way he looked lying on the living room floor with that awful gurgling sound leaking out of his mouth. Ponytail turns to look at me with narrowed eyes and mismatched eyebrows. I should look away as if embarrassed by the favor.

"Sit tight, sister!"

Phew, thanks! You're a lover all right. The bike peels off. My fingers dig into the leather. The bike's wheels plough into the dirt shoulder and climb up barriers that have just been redone. We fly above the cars like superheroes who just sprouted wings. The barrier crumbles under the wheels as we go and—*bam!*—right before hitting the school gates we soar like perfection and land back on the road. Ponytail turns around and winks. He weaves through the sidewalk and, again, we get stuck in a knot of cars.

He turns to shoot me a bummed-out look. I wink. He presses his lips together and runs the bike down the cliffside like it's a camel. Easy now. He's taking this a little too seriously, I feel like my brain's about to drop into my throat. Rocks scatter beneath the wheels, and due to Newton's Second Law or maybe the Third, the seat of the bike strikes a deadly blow against my ass. I start listing off every pro biker I can think of plus their aunts and uncles and third cousins and repeat it twice over until we finally reach the bottom.

We pass under the bridge and zigzag up cramped alleyways. He knows the streets so well it's clear he's either from here or plays here like me. He climbs up the uphills and takes fickle byways and backroads on the way down. If Emo Ali were around he'd say something like, *Respect man, Darakeh's a fucking labyrinth! What was your friend's name again—Borges? Have him drop by sometime.*

"Here we are, Khoddami Street . . . Shit, what've they done to you!"

Ponytail's twisted around to fix his worried eyes on one side of my face, which now twitters beneath his kind gaze. Boy, where did you learn to look at people like that?

"Put some ice on it when you get there."

And with that you give yourself away—you're one of those prissy kids, or else you'd spare me that kind, compassionate look and say, *Take a few drags when you get there and you're good.*

His eyes run up and down my face. It's like he's actually worried. Damn, I miss him already. That look! I wish I could forget about the high and about Ashkan and Nana Molouk and Sara. I get off the bike and slap a quality smile across my face.

"You're too kind."

I punch him on the bicep then bow and hold out my

palms like I owe him or whatever. He keeps looking at me, worried.

"You sure you don't want me to take you all the way there? Where do they live exactly?"

He's pretty and I know it and today's a good day for loving. Too bad I'm sober. If I weren't—if Nana Molouk . . . if Sara . . . if . . . then I'd climb on the back of your bike and we'd go for a ride.

"Are you sure you don't need any help? I mean, like a ride to a hospital or something?"

This is starting to get pathetic. He shifts a new match that's just materialized out of nowhere from one side of his lips to the other and gives me a look that's supposedly worried but actually traced with mischief. Boy, today's no day for loving!

I stretch out a hand.

"Thanks."

"Well if you need anything, happy to help. Kiarash Noshouni—just say the name around Bakhsh Square and they'll tell you where to find me."

A 180-degree turn and a wink, and at the edge of his jackal-jawed smile, the gold tooth gleams.

Latif opens the door but not with the usual smile and bowed head. His eyes flutter.

"Miss Shadi! This is the end!" He wipes the tears at the corners of his eyes with a handkerchief. "They'll be left for dead. If it's like this here, then just think—"

He sobs into the handkerchief then looks up to stare straight into my eyes. I should say something. Something, anything. Something to calm him down a little, to get rid of that twitch in his eyes and give them back their usual smile. But my tongue's tied. Like I've gone mute.

"This is the end!"

His knees give out. He plops down and beats his head with the handkerchief.

"Is Sara home?"

"Yes, miss. But Mr. Siamak left early in the morning. Mr. Ali is in, and Miss Shahnaz left just before you arrived—I believe she was angry. Mr. Mazyar I don't know, and Mr. Ashkan's been out since last night. As for Miss Sara, the lady's been making music all day."

It's impressive Latif still has a handle on the occupancy rate around here.

"Get up, Latif, everything's fine. These half-assed tremors—I mean, you can hardly call that an earthquake."

Latif doesn't move. He's squatting down holding a handkerchief to his head, staring into space. I squat down next to him. A few months ago I'd cast a spell, talking to him about this and that. Now my mind works like a charm but my jaw won't budge. What do I say? If only I could preach like Mazyar does, say something like, *Life goes on*, or maybe more like, *What's so great about life anyway that's got you holding on so tight?* Or if only I could explain to him, logically, reasonably, like Rahim would, that this earthquake has just hit Tehran and has nothing to do with anywhere else, let alone Afghanistan. My jaw won't budge.

He keeps staring at the dry leaves in the garden with those green eyes of his that now look a little yellow and soon swell with beads of tears that slide down his leathery cheeks. He is and isn't here. I reach into the pocket of my backpack and press a blister pack of Tylenol 3 into his palm.

"Take two or three of these, get in bed, and you'll feel better."

If he takes two or three, he'll sleep for two days straight. That one time he caught a cold and Rahim gave him codeine, he was high for three. He won't move. Like they've screwed him to the ground. I give him a friendly pound on the shoulder and half rise so he'll get up too. He doesn't.

Bach's Invention no. 8 sounds from the house. As Latif likes to say, the lady's making music. When it gets to measure six the music stops then starts over. Each time the composition gets stuck one or two notes earlier or later, then again from the top. If I had to listen to Sara practicing all day, I'd go insane.

She's sitting at the old out-of-tune piano like usual, mashing down the pedal and making the windows of the Kolah Farangi Emirate shake. Sara, when did you come back? Ever since first grade you've been there beside me. At my desk or me at yours. On the seesaw or on the swings. In the big black car that used to pick you up. Or in this very garden, playing hide-and-seek, laughing, laughing, laughing. So when did you disappear? You went to Paris then all of a sudden the sorrow of exile seized you and like a ghost you popped up in the crates of herbs and tomatoes for sale at Tajrish Square. So that I said to myself, see how all that hash is finally catching up to you? See how you've become melancholic and hallucinate in broad daylight? Sara, in the middle of Tajrish Square? After all these years?

She doesn't ease off the keys until I put a hand on her shoulder. Except for that tuneless piano she can't hear a thing. She turns and throws herself into my arms with the usual thin smile.

"Shadi!"

I want time to stop. I want to look at her thin pale lips and her downcast black eyes and her thin crescent eyebrows forever. At the foolishness or love or affection that flutters in her eyes. I wrap my arms around her and dig my nose into her hair. The pines of our childhood spin around me. She takes my face between her hands and looks at me through wet, frowning eyes.

"Arash said you were up a tree when they found you."

She frowns even deeper.

"Is it true?"

I dig my nose into her hair again and smell the pines.

"Let it go, Sara."

She tilts her head and purses her lips.

"So I went a little too far," I say.

"A little?"

"I fucked up I fucked up I fucked up. Don't frown."

She holds me.

"My crazy little dirtbag."

"Where's Siamak?"

She pulls my beanie off and digs her fingers into my scalp.

"Don't know. When I woke up he was already gone."

I get up.

"In that case he'll turn up in no time. He can't survive more than a couple hours without you."

She gives me a look. As if to say, *You mean it's just another habit?* Or, *Shadi, et tu?*

Seriously, me too? I mean, I'm your oldest friend, I'm—why can't I say it? Say what? What *can* I say to you, dumbass?

"What, you won't do me the honor of firing up that stone age torch when Siamak's not around?"

Her smile spreads to her eyes.

"Bitch."

The ground slips out from under our feet. She lays her head on my chest and covers her ears. The windows in the foyer dance Bandari. Any second now the chandelier will break free from the ceiling. Sara trembles in my arms. She's like a fish with just a thin veil of fat wrapped around her delicate bones. An earthquake isn't so bad with Sara in one's arms. I hug her harder. Maybe if I press you close the earth will come to rest.

"Calm down," I say. "Hush."

It goes calm and quiet. I take her face between my hands. Her eyes are still shut.

"It's over."

She lifts her eyelids slowly. Like she's afraid that when she opens her eyes nothing will be where it belongs. She looks around. First at the shitty grand piano.

"Don't worry, it's good for another earthquake or two."

She glares.

"Where is everyone? They're not dead, are they?"

She untangles herself from my arms.

"They're asleep."

"Asleep? Seriously? You people wouldn't come out of your caves if a nuke went off."

"I'm worried about Siamak."

"He's a grown man, can't he take care of himself? He should be worried about you after leaving you here all alone . . . Where'd he go anyway?"

"I don't know. He was pacing all last night, then in the morning he was gone. What if something happens to him?"

"Yeah you *should* be worried—the Siamak I know is at

an auntie's right now reclining under a warm quilt by a coal korsi in a tribal tent sucking on an opium pacifier."

She turns her head and smiles as she goes down the stairs.

"You're jealous."

"Yes, I am."

She takes a key out of the cardigan Grammy Dearest knit for her. You and your beloved's temple, the only room in this house with a door that locks. Now that Siamak's gone I can lie on the tattered carpeting with my head on your lap and let loose.

"Will you do it? I want to see what it's like to get Siamak's royal treatment for once."

She gives me a look.

"Fuck off, like I've never lit a pipe for you?"

"Well yeah, except now Siamak's not around to count the drags. You really should give some thought to the parsimony of your lover. And quit digging through all those jewelry boxes, there's no way he's left a single dab behind."

"He never takes much with him."

"This time's different. Or at least he's not leaving it anywhere you can find. You're too open—open heart, open hand."

Her soft white hands open and close each of the wooden and inlaid and engraved and bas-relief boxes. If your great-grandmother was as kind and white and supple as you are then no wonder she was Naseeruddin Shah's favorite.

"Hold on."

She pushes a small armoire aside and removes the baseboard behind it.

"Whoa, Miss Marple! Found his stash?"

She opens a matchbox.

"It's my fucking stash . . . Shit, I've only got two balls left."

She tucks the box back into the hole, replaces the baseboard, and pushes the armoire back into place.

"What, why are you looking at me like that?"

I'm speechless. I can't believe Sara has her own stash.

"So you've been in withdrawal before?"

She sits down cross-legged on a cushion and puts the ball on a pin.

"No. But it can't hurt for a rainy day."

She gives a little laugh and winks.

I lay my head on a pillow and take the bubbling pipe between my teeth. What a dream, looking at your face from down here. She applies the nail. I hold in the smoke. Close my eyes. I want to soak it up with every single cell in my body. The Colonel's head appears before my eyes—I want to tell you the story about Ashkan and the Colonel. But no, maybe you'll get up and go. I don't want you to move.

"Shadi! What's happening?"

"What do you care?"

"Oh, I don't know."

You don't know? When you sit on this cushion and light the burner for your darling Siamak, what do you care if the earth is dancing Bandari or not? When Siamak's got the pipe between his lips and he's stealing your heart with his bewitching eyes then what difference does it make if the ground switches places with the sky?

"I'm worried about Siamak."

If only Siamak would never come back. If only I could lie here like this forever and you could talk with me like you talk with him forever.

"I fucking hate Siamak, you know that?"

"Riiight."

You stretch it out long like you're not in the mood for my nonsense. I suck in the smoke. I suck. I suck—I can't breathe. So you're used to Siamak's drags? Forgot I can't take such long hits? I let go of the pipe.

"Oh sorry, too long?"

Don't talk to me like that. So distant? So formal? I close my eyes. I swallow the smoke. Tomorrow or maybe the day after tomorrow I'll let it out. I want to keep it there. Always, forever.

"Arash said they found you stuck in a tree like some fucking frog."

"Arash is full of shit."

"Yeah, fuck you."

You pick up the nail. Damn, you're out of it—I still haven't let out my last hit. Your heart's not in it. You're barely here. Is this how you do it for Siamak?

"So why the tree?"

"I was flying."

"On your private jet?"

"On something . . ."

The nail and safety pin remain suspended in the air

so she can laugh at me good and hard and press her lips to my forehead.

"My little piece of shit."

The cool wet of her lips lingers on my forehead. I close my eyes.

"What were you on?"

"Don't remember."

"Who were you with?"

"Don't remember."

She cracks up again and digs her nose in my hair.

"My lovely little turd."

I drop the pipe.

Her hands stay suspended in the air like she's operating on a patient who's suddenly come to.

"Are you done?"

"Yup."

"What's your problem?"

"Where do I start?"

She turns off the torch and sweeps her hair forward over my face.

"None for you?" I ask.

"No."

Now we're stretched out, heads brushing on the same pillow, bodies pointing in opposite directions. The afternoon sun shines through the narrow basement windows and covers us in stripes. I raise my hands. She raises her hands. Remember? Those times in the garden in the leaves. We'd spin so much that the plane trees kept spinning when we stopped to stick our heads together and hook our hands together and talk about our dreams. And how it's like we're still spinning.

"You always wanted to travel the world," I say. "A whole long list of weird places."

She locks her fingers in my fingers even tighter.

"You wanted to find a husband and name your daughter Aisha."

I crack up. You crack up. I laugh harder. You laugh harder. I spin. You spin.

"How would it make you feel if a quality earthquake hit right now and buried the two of us here?" I ask.

"I'll go anywhere with you."

"Like old times?"

"Like old times."

Your eyes twinkle with laughter and promise you're telling the truth. You were always game back then too. I used to come up with the craziest ideas and you were still game. Hanging from the rope in the garden well. Sneaking out through the old broken gate to discover strange places. I was always the one who got a beating. Or two, one on my count and one on yours. Right when we were getting somewhere you'd start gushing tears and I'd have to try to figure everything out alone until Latif or Miss Gelin found us and Maman gave me a good beating while you simply took your repose in your grandfather's big, warm arms, watching until she dragged me home and then the next day you'd ask, *Did it hurt?*

You jump up and laugh.

"Remember that time we stole Bobak's backpack and burned all his books?"

"Yeah—I was locked in the pantry for a whole day until Nana Molouk rescued me."

"You do realize it was all because of Nana Molouk that your mom beat you like that?"

"You do realize it was all because of a thousand different things. And now it all makes me sick."

I take her soft hands and put them on my cheeks.

"I wish you'd never left. Or that you hadn't met Siamak when you got back."

"Shadi, Siamak is an angel."

"Yeah, with those fucking airs of his. Long wavy hair, curlicue beard, round eyes that'll outlast Persepolis. If he didn't have that preclassic thing going, would you still have fallen in love with him?"

"Siamak is kind."

"Riiight."

Her fingers crawl through my spiky hair.

"Why don't you fall in love?"

"Tried, didn't work out."

She frowns.

"Meaning what?"

"I sent twenty-two lovey-dovey texts to all the boys I know one afternoon."

"And?"

"I mean."

"The results, if you please."

"Two fuck-offs, three forget-about-its, three people ghosted, and three phone numbers for a shrink."

She purses her thin lips.

"You're definitely crazy."

"Do you know how lucky you are that your parents are dead and gone?"

"Bullshit. Wish you were in my place?"

"Absolutely. What a dream! You're born in prison, then they hand you over to your rich and kind grandparents."

"Yeah, it's been great."

"So you'd rather have my mom for a mother? Or try a dad like Ashkan and Elham's, who abandons you and up and moves to the other side of the world?"

Shahnaz materializes in the doorway. She's taking shallow breaths and her nostrils flare in and out. She purses her lips and then—

"Rahim took everything with him."

Seriously? Shahnaz slumps down and starts bawling. Sara gets up and gently puts a hand on her shoulder. Don't, you fool! Shahnaz pounces on her like a panther. There's no telling friend from foe when she gets hysterical like this. Before I can save Sara from getting truly pummeled she's tasted three or four punches. Shahnaz eases off her and starts up the stairs, making her way through a laundry list of curses at our mothers and fathers and sisters as she goes.

Sara's hair is a mess. Tears stream down her face. I take her face between my hands. There's an imprint of Shahnaz's ring on her cheeks.

"Stupid. You know you can't go near that bitch when she loses it."

She snorts back her snot and pouts like a child. Crashing, smashing sounds come from upstairs. We run up the stairs two by two. Afsoon and Payam are standing by the door to their room with groggy eyes. Shahnaz is in the parlor screaming and foaming at the mouth.

She throws her slippers at the window. She rips up the sheet music resting on the piano. If only she'd take it all out on the music. She marches into Rahim's room, takes his clothes out of the closet piece by piece, and rips them in half. She bangs the glass medicine cabinet open and shut. So it's actually empty? But Rahim isn't a shit like Siamak to just ditch like that. Emo Ali comes out of his room, jeans hanging off his ass.

Now Shahnaz takes Rahim's big umbrella and smashes the glass while cursing us filthy bitches out. Sara screams and cries. Shahnaz has moved on to the pocket mirrors, the same ones she brought back for Rahim after every trip. I push Sara into Ali's arms: "Take her downstairs."

Emo Ali takes Sara by the hand and pulls her down the stairs. Mazyar's standing in the door to his room in his underwear, watching and looking confused.

Shahnaz marches out of Rahim's room holding a shard of mirror, her yellow eyes practically popping out of their sockets. She looks back and forth between me and Mazyar, like she can't decide who to rip into first. Emo Ali runs back upstairs. Shahnaz lunges at Mazyar. Mazyar dodges.

"Somebody stop her crazy ass!"

Shahnaz chases Mazyar, who makes a run for it out to the courtyard. Shahnaz fixes on Payam and Afsoon.

Payam shoves Afsoon back into their room and slams the door.

"Somebody call Rahim!"

When Shahnaz hears his name she ramps up the crazy. She lunges at Payam with the mirror shard aimed at his jugular. Emo Ali flies and clutches her hand from behind and squeezes until the shard falls from her grip, then floors her with a left hook. He sits on her chest, wrings her neck, and presses down. Shahnaz's face goes red, goes blue . . . Any second now her eyes are actually about to pop out of their sockets. Her legs flail in the air. Her hands clench Ali's hands and try to pry them off her neck. Now Latif arrives like an angel sent from the skies. He plucks Emo Ali off Shahnaz and tosses him into the corner like a puppet. Now Shahnaz is lying there in a fetal position, sobbing.

"Well, my friends, allow yourselves a sigh of relief. The patient has entered her depressive mode and won't rebound for another twenty-four hours."

That comes from Mazyar. He's still half-naked, bent over Shahnaz and studying her like she's some lab rat. Latif is still wide-eyed, staring at Emo Ali, who mutters, "What, why are you looking at me like that?"

Latif grumbles under his breath as he walks out.

"It's the end of the world—there's no mercy even between Muslims."

Why is everything going to shit today? I glance over at Sara. There's a smile creeping behind her eyes too. We both crack up. I seriously can't believe Emo Ali was about to choke Shahnaz to death. I put a hand on his shoulder.

"What the hell got into you, boy?"

Emo Ali stalks off with his jeans hanging down past his ass like he doesn't give a fuck.

"She's just messing with us, the fucking psycho!"

He slams the door. The windows in the foyer shake. Payam and Afsoon slam their door too. These entitled motherfuckers, nobody owes them shit. Mazyar grabs Shahnaz by the arms and drags her into her room then shuts the door.

"A corpse should never be left out."

"Amen," I say. "Now make me a cup of tea and you'd really do it for me."

"Shut up, slut."

He slams the kitchen door behind him.

"You want some tea?" Sara asks.

"I'm just messing."

I pull a cigarette out of pocket #220 of my cargos.

"What key is this in?"

She's trying to find the right chords for an old Armenian tune that Grammy Dearest used to hum. I search through my pockets. Which one of Newton's laws was it that says keep your cigarette and lighter within thirty centimeters at all times?

"How come none of these chords sound right?"

Is it possible there's a lighter hiding somewhere in the seams of this ripped-up chaise? Crassus! Where are you when I need you? They're killing your uncle.

"Ugh!" Sara groans.

"Why is there a psycho camped out in every nook and cranny of this house?"

"So there's an F-sharp in it but then G major sounds off?"

"The D-sharps don't count for anything?"

"Ohh . . . E minor?"

I find a shitty green lighter between the cushions and I'm as happy as Archimedes.

"Is this part okay?"

She gets the melody right but the chords run as gracefully as a crab. I swirl the smoke around in my mouth and let it out in rings.

"Why can't I get it right . . ."

"So Shahnaz lost it when her dad died?" I say.

"Poor thing. You'd lose it too if your dad died like that."

"I'll be okay no matter how my parents die."

"E minor? You sure?"

"Who knows what that bastard Rahim gives her to set her off like that."

"Easy, Shadi. Rahim and Siamak are related."

"Oh right, for a second I forgot that this place is royal court for all the indigenous tribes and nomadic peoples of Shiraz, Isfahan, and the province of Kohgiluyeh and Boyer-Ahmad."

"Shahnaz does better with Rahim around."

"I'm sure, given all those pills he feeds through her umbilical cord."

"It sounded different when Grammy sang it . . ."

"Why doesn't she go back home?"

"Because she can't be going at it with her insane mom 24/7. Think about it! They take your dad's naked corpse and throw it in the trash."

"Yeah, it must be awful—Daddy pops a Viagra, has a heart attack in his lover's arms, gets stuffed in the dumpster by said lover, and then to top it all off your mom's batshit crazy . . . Hey, here's an idea, maybe it's genetic."

"That's cold. Remember how smart she was when we were kids?"

"So smart people don't go crazy?"

"Remember those big, honeyed eyes?"

"Five minutes ago those same honeyed eyes were tearing us apart."

"She's just so alone."

"What the hell does that have to do with you? Why is it your problem that her dad's dead or her mom's insane? Just 'cause she was cute when we were kids doesn't mean she should move in with you."

"Without Rahim around we'd all starve."

"Starve or stay sober?"

"Get over here and figure this out already! Didn't you learn anything all those years in college?"

"I didn't learn shit in college."

She pulls my hand to get me up from the chaise. The off-key keys make me feel good. I put the cigarette at the corner of my lips and let my eyelids droop.

"I fucking love this piano."

"What about it?"

"Everything. The fact that nothing's how it should

be. Listen to this C major." *Dongggg*. "How about a post-modern atonal concert, shall I?"

She looks at me with eyes that play at being pissed.

"How is it my fault that Grammy Dearest wasn't as off pitch as this piano?"

She sits next to me and pulls my hair.

"Figure it out."

"How, by pulling it out of my—here, look." I play a few chords.

She throws herself at me.

"Where's Siamak?"

She starts sobbing.

"Why won't he come back?"

I lay the cigarette at the edge of the piano. With one hand I stroke her hair, which lies fanned across my chest, and with the other I bang out a few funky jazz chords. She pulls away to flop onto the chaise and dig her face into the pillows. It'll be a good hour before the tears stop.

"Quit it. You can't last an hour without Siamak before you start whining like a little bitch."

"Shut up," she mutters in a nasally voice.

"Shut up," I mutter in a nasally voice.

Charades! That'll cheer her up. I stand up, click my heels to the floor, raise my arms in the air, and spin in a lame imitation of flamenco. She sobs and her shoulders shake.

I drop my voice an octave and do an impression of the lead singer from Kiosk.

"*The night is imprisoned in your tresses*

"Compared to you the moon needs finessing

"Stay here tonight, it's too late to go

"Your voice is a song and your eyes are angelic

"Nice, I'm diggin' it, my lies are poetic."

She looks up and glares at me through wet eyes. I shake my ass and thrust; she just dies for Elvis.

"This is what livin' is. Pimping out the stereo

"What are you up to this weekend–

"Shemshak or Dizin, where do we go?"

A bitter smile settles at the corner of her lips. I need to try harder. I pick the tempo up, lift my knees higher, shake my ass harder.

"Manliness is this

"Bench press ripped chest–

"Can't call yourself a man without rims."

I lift the neck of my electric guitar like I'm finishing off the riff and–

"*Bwng!*" I belt out the chords.

She stares at me unimpressed and tosses me a sorry smile. I need to put more feeling into it. I furrow my eyebrows and croon like Elvis and lift her chin with my finger to gaze languidly into her eyes like I'm serenading her with the greatest love song that ever was.

"That won't cut it, good looks and a fortune

"It's also about the accent, this way sounds foreign."

And with that she finally bursts out laughing.

"You're an idiot."

I scrunch my brows in concentration and play a long, difficult riff on the neck of my fake guitar. I pick up the tempo.

"Summers in Marmaris

"Winters at the slopes."

I whip my head back and forth and throw myself around like some crazy hard-rock frontman who's bouncing off the walls.

"Plastic parts and colored contact lenses

"Who cares where you're headed when you're riding in Benzes."

You get up and shimmy and shake with me.

"What're you up to this weekend?

"Day and night we're on a bender

"Night and day we're popping pills

"Daddy's got your back, babe, no worries, all thrills."

The earth slips out from under our feet. The windows shake. You scream. You press your head into my chest, you scream . . . You scream. You scream. You scream.

I open my eyes. Sara's head is on my lap. There's a soft whistling as her nostrils flare. A poor excuse for Sasy Mankan's sweet vocals floats over from the kitchen courtesy of Mazyar. He never does pull it off. There's such a racket of pots and pans going you'd think he's feeding an army. At least someone around here can still feel hunger. Bach's Mass in B Minor seeps out of Emo Ali's room. All the dipshit ever listens to is that sad song and doom metal then he's got a finger up his ass wondering why he's depressed.

I gently lift Sara's head and lay it on the sofa. She turns to her side, tucks her hands under her head, and starts snoring. I push her hair out of her face and caress her cheek. A faint smile settles on her lips. Must be dreaming that Siamak's the one leaning over her.

I pull on my army jacket and pick up my backpack. I need to leave. I don't have the patience for the fit she's going to have when she wakes up and realizes her darling Siamak's still gone. Siamak is not coming back. Rahim is not coming back. All the motherfucking cowards are making a break for it. Mazyar's bent over the stove in his underwear, cradling the phone between his head and shoulder. He stirs the pot as he chews the fat. Good thing the cord on that fossilized phone could stretch all the way out to the courtyard.

"Heyyyy."

When Sara's darling grandpapa was shopping for a kitchen phone way back when, he must've foreseen the day his house would become a clubhouse for a bunch of freeloading tail-chasing floozyflirts. And he must have known that said floozyflirt squatters would want to flirt with their floozies while whipping up something for lunch.

"Aw, baaabe . . ."

I throw my backpack down on a chair, head for the phone mount, and hit the switch hook.

"Miss you . . ."

This last sentiment sounds in a vacuum. I pull the phone out from under his chin.

"Bitch, what the hell?"

He's wrist-deep in a sink full of dirty dishes and moldy leftovers and shit-brown bubbles.

"What the fuck is wrong with you?"

I walk back over and dial home.

"Fucking bitch."

On the second ring Bobak's voice echoes in my ears.

"Shadi! Maman and I are taking off." Pause. "Baba's

meeting us there." Pause. "Come as soon as you can, please." Pause. "We're worried about you . . . Please." *Beep*. Gracias por llamar.

Bobak left a message just for me. All for me. I hit Redial.

"Shadi! Maman and I are taking off . . ."

Maman and I? Baba's meeting us there? And you want me to come with you? Just forget about everyone else? About Nana Molouk and Arash and–shit, they probably didn't even take Miss Gelin with them. I dial again.

"What, they're screening calls?"

There's something off about Bobak's voice. Makes me want to vomit but I can't put my finger on it. It doesn't sound like him. There's something different about it–something god-awful and different.

"Shadi! Maman and . . ."

He sounds weird. Like he hit Record right after stuffing his face with hot fries.

"Please."

His voice isn't shaking. There's no fear in it. Instead there's something else. Something fucking else . . . Wait. All the magic's gone! It's hollow.

"Please."

Hollow as a soap bubble.

"Please."

I put the phone down and pick up my backpack.

"Have a nice chat?"

"Shut the fuck up."

A wet saucepan hits the doorframe.

Latif isn't in the garden. He's not in his room off the

courtyard either. I open the gates. Crassus is sitting on the other side.

"Hey, boy, what are you doing here?"

I pick him up. He digs his nose into my chest acting cute.

"So you're giving up on Ashkan too?"

He whimpers.

"Don't tell me you're here for me? I'm not going back there."

He looks at me.

"I don't think you want to go back there either. Come on, let's go."

Crassus leads the way, wagging his tail pleased as punch. Lucky him, he's such a cutie. The square's filled to the brim with people, like a steaming bowl of aush that's about to spill over. People are practically climbing over each other. A volley of roadhouse cursing comes from somewhere in the crowd.

"Fight! Let's go check it out, Crassus."

I climb onto the hood of a rickety Paykan. Can't see a thing. I climb onto the roof. Now that's more like it. I sit cross-legged and rest my chin on my hands. Mr. Qolam has taken center stage in the middle of Darakeh Square. Like those old-time wrestlers who used to tear steel chains with their bare hands. Dressed the part in long boxers and a ratty undershirt, he paces this way and that way and screws up half his face and roars. Crassus hops up onto the Paykan and rests his muzzle on my lap, making himself at home.

Mr. Reza and Mr. Fatahi and the rest of the guys are

standing skewer-straight in front of their shops with the gates pulled down. Mr. Qolam paces this way and that way machete in hand, bellowing some sorry refrain at three pineapple head kids he's got tied down by his feet. A voice I recognize calls from across the square, "Stand up! Stand up."

Parvin's got hold of the herb peddler's truck and she's chanting slogans into the ancient mic with her voice dropped an octave and her feet stomping to the beat. As soon as Crassus sees her, he jumps up and starts sprinting.

"Get back here, you'll get lost!"

Parvin's a little off-key but her voice still has its old warmth and richness. If she and Maman had only joined the college choir instead of the leftists when the revolution happened, we'd have a couple Pavarottis by now.

A handful of kids are gathered around the truck staring at Parvin with dropped jaws. But Mr. Qolam's putting on the better show. He's got those three skinny-ass boys roped together as he marches and roars. Poor things were probably caught catcalling some girl, and today's a good day for playing the hero. I feel bad for the boys. There's no sign of the regular police or the riot police, they must be busy somewhere else. Still, if it takes them any longer this lunatic might actually use his machete to make pineapple chuck chop.

Everybody's just standing there watching. Cowards. The boys' eyes dart back and forth like sacrificial lambs. Mr. Qolam sears the air with his machete and curses and screws up half his face over and over again. If only he didn't have that ridiculous tic he could've landed a wife and made a man of himself so he could stop fretting over everyone else's chastity.

Mr. Qolam's got his back turned when one of the pineapple heads quietly manages to get up and make a run for it. Mr. Qolam chases after him. The other two run the other way deep into the crowd. Mr. Qolam turns around and chases after them. He whips the machete over his head and runs. Let it go, idiot. With that fine figure of yours, there's no way you're catching them.

Mr. Qolam and his bear of a belly don't even make it to the roundabout. He lets go of the machete and starts pounding on any youths within reach, who then charge him throwing punches left and right. A veritable King Kong, Mr. Qolam stands tall with seven, eight, maybe ten guys hanging off him. Finally they knock him down and go at him tooth and nail. King Kong–like roars sound from somewhere in the crowd but there's no sign of the man himself. The boys hoot and holler and jump up and down. They must've creamed him. A few of them get caught up in the heat of the moment and start destroying everything in sight. They smash the windows on a minibus then rock it back and forth until it tips.

Parvin's still standing on the roof of the truck yelling chants into the mic but Crassus is nowhere to be found. Hope he's okay? Shit, I'm staying up here.

The bus ticket kiosk goes next. One of the youths sounds a rebel yell and charges at Mr. Reza's shop, holding Mr. Qolam's machete. Mr. Reza tries to make a break for it but instead gets plowed.

His shopwindows are smashed to smithereens and not only the youths but old men and women are rushing in to loot the shelves. The butcher shopwindows and the greengrocer windows are next to go. How they manage to unlock the security gates is beyond me. Some little old lady's got a lamb shank tucked under her arm and she's moving fast. Across the square the windows of the farmers' co-op get smashed. They don't even spare Old Man Hamzeh's dry goods kiosk. Crassus leaps onto the hood of the car.

"Back already? I told you not to go out there . . . Pretty cool shitstorm, huh?"

He looks at me worried.

"Aw it's okay, boy, it's nothing really."

I pull his head in close and stroke his stinky black fur. Down below, two baldies grab onto the same bucket of rice and pull. One of them lets go of the bucket and hooks a left under the other one's jaw. The guy goes *splat* on the ground. Baldy no. 1 grabs the bucket of rice and starts off, but no. 2 gets himself back up, grabs no. 1 by the collar and lands a right hook smack on the jaw.

"Look, Crassus. It's fucking amazing, straight out of *Easy Street*."

Crassus whimpers and nuzzles into me.

"You lame wuss."

Three choppers circle overhead. Over the loudspeaker everyone is invited to remain calm. They hover closer. The wind from the rotors sends everything flying. You can't even see your own feet. A dust storm picks up.

"Time to go, Crassus. Everyone's about to clear out and we'll be the only two losers left to arrest."

I hop onto the hood and then down off the car. I sling my backpack over my shoulder and take Crassus in my arms. The air's swirling with so much shit it makes you wonder where all that orange peel and newspaper even came from. Like one of those fake storms in the movies. Three minibuses followed by Mercedes cop cars make their way uphill through the square. The officers start pouring out. I duck my face behind the collar of my army jacket and quietly pass through the crowd of people running in every direction. This way they won't stop me. All I have to do is stay calm. Like I'm walking over a sea of people and I have to be careful not to step on anyone. While holding my breath. If I focus hard enough no one will see me. I'll become invisible. I try to duck even farther behind my collar and keep my eyes on my shoes. On my tennis shoes. On the knotted laces of my tennis shoes. On that shoelace that's been twisted around so it dangles off to the right on one of my tennis shoes. People pass by me like meteorites. Batons swing up. I dig my fingers into Crassus's fur and scratch him around the ears. His heart's beating as fast as a sparrow's. Poor thing's about to have a heart attack. Calm down, darling. Nothing's going to happen to us. We're almost done crossing the square. Everyone's leaving us alone. A million lunatics to choose from, they hardly know we're here. Keep your nose buried in my chest. Just like that. And don't open your eyes. Try putting your paws over your ears to block out the screams. Soon we'll find us a nice little spot on some side street to lie down and have a cigarette. Some ten or fifteen Green Suits are dragging Mr. Qolam along the ground by the arms and legs. Mr. Qolam kicks and snorts like a raging bull. Pineapple heads and pretty boys run like sheep loose from the flock and Green Suits herd them onto minibuses like shepherds. Nobody comes after me. Nobody sees me.

I drop my backpack and slump down onto the ground. Crassus opens his eyes just a sliver. His eyes dart left and right.

"What, can't believe I got us out? Your dude knows what's up."

Crassus looks up the road and whimpers.

"What?"

He looks at me sadly.

"You're not worried about Parvin?"

He looks at me sadly.

"I'm not going after her."

He whimpers.

"Absolutely not."

He barks.

"Let it go. She's out there living her best life. When was the last time she got to chant those slogans? And any second now she's about to get arrested, and then she'll really be living it up."

He looks at me sadly.

"Attaboy, don't worry. Who knows, with any luck they'll put her in the cell next to Nana Molouk and they can keep each other company."

He rests his head on my chest.

"Now that's more like it."

I reach into pocket #304 of my cargos and pull out the matchbox. Only two balls left.

"Look, Crassus, this here represents the last of our provisions. I'm throwing it back and then—"

Shouting and the sound of boots pounding pavement. Crassus sits up and perks his ears. Three or four pineapple heads have made it halfway down the street. Guess they don't realize it's a dead end and now there's nothing to do but turn around. A Green Suit turns the corner, grabs one in one hand and two in the other, and pulls.

"See, he left us alone just like I said. We're invisible."

Crassus lays his head on my stomach and I lay the opium balls under my tongue. My mouth is dry. I suck. They won't melt. I ball up my spit and scoop them onto my tongue.

Fuck me. Why did I think I could count on Rahim and Siamak. The dealers who hang around Pilas Park have more integrity than those two bastards. I mean, Rahim? That fucker—seriously, what kind of a fool thinks you can count on a kid from Abadan?

The same kind of fool who goes fishing for a high in Ashkan's stomach lining. Who thinks Rahim and Siamak will stay home on a day like today to share. Who abandons Sara to a house full of psychos.

I suck. The bitterness finally gets damp. I push them back under my tongue. Keep sucking. Crassus, my dear, never forget Newton's First Law: No thinking when you're sober. Wait. Wait. Wait. For the bitterness to go down. Solves all the world's problems.

I suck and push the bitterness down. My fingers walk through Crassus's fur. Everything's going to work out just fine. Crassus rolls over and digs his snout into my side.

"Enough. Stop acting cute."

I suck and swallow. My stomach warms up. The little creature starts at my toes and makes its way up. Rahim and Siamak, that was a mistake. I should never have counted on those two coming through. Uncle Asadollah or Uncle Mamdal, now *they* would've been the ones to go to. Hell, anyone in Maman's poker crew and I would've been better off. Old-timers do a person right. Don't leave you hanging at the very least. I keep sucking. The little creature comes up slow and steady. Passes through my knees and pulls itself up. Old-timers know the score. They've always got a solid hundred grams stashed away somewhere in case of emergency. Uncle Mamdal's definitely got a pack or two of Senators tucked away somewhere in a safe, just one loosie and all debts are forgiven. I keep sucking. The little creature's all the way up to my quads. Any second now it'll pull itself up and leap into my pelvis. Explode into a thousand pieces. Then the tadpoles in my stomach will swim laps.

If it weren't for Ashkan and that damn savior complex of mine, I'd be sitting here with a good twenty-five grams in my pocket by now. What did I think this was, a Fardin flick? Bullshit. Truth is I went to Ashkan's *for* the twenty-five grams. But the bastard had already seen to it himself.

And after that? Why did I go looking for Siamak? Well, why not? How was I supposed to know that fucker would leave his own girlfriend in a lurch? Guess I thought he wouldn't leave me hanging like this, even if only as a courtesy to his girl. I suck and swallow. The tadpoles swim upstream.

I shouldn't have left Sara there all alone. When she comes down and realizes I'm not there—shit, what if Shahnaz wakes up and goes crazy again? Why didn't I think of Uncle Asadollah sooner? If I'd gone straight to him this morning he would've spared me a few balls. And I could've hit up Uncle Mamdal right after. And then Uncle Habib. Four balls from each of them and . . . Four balls won't kill anyone. I keep sucking. The tadpoles swim up through my chest and neck then throw themselves into my head. My head heats up. My jaw heats up.

"Come here, Crassus, come hold me. Any second now these gears will get cranking . . ."

The tadpoles swim through my head. I shouldn't have left Sara there all alone. The sound of screaming comes from far far away.

"What do you think, did they take Miss Gelin with them?"

Bobak left a message on the machine all for me. Just for me. Crassus rolls over and digs his nose into my neck.

"Stop it, slut. So selfish."

He whimpers.

"Why didn't you stay home with Ashkan?"

He lifts his head and looks at me sadly.

"Think Uncle Asadollah and them stuck it out?"

The tadpoles swim laps in my skull. I want a cigarette but don't have it in me to reach into my pockets to get one. One deep breath in and the tadpoles will sprout wings.

"If I'd gone straight there I would've found them. That fucking bastard Rahim."

A helicopter whirs overhead. I suck. I swallow.

"Maybe I'm good . . . Maybe the big one will hit right now and bingo, game over. The earth will crack open. Or this brick wall right here will collapse and crush us . . . I wish I was at home. Would've been nice to be crushed in my own room, by my own bricks, you know . . . Bitch, stop being a diva. What difference does it make. Bricks are bricks."

I suck. I swallow. The tadpoles swim. Swim laps in my skull. Swim. Swim. Swim.

The slimy wet on my lips is cold. The wet on my body is cold . . . Smells like shit—no, not quite. Smells like moldy leftovers. Smells like rotten oranges. Smells like an alcoholic's diarrhea. Smells like cheese. Like mulberries. Like smoke. Like raspberries. Like Crassus . . . If I just open my eyes. Just lift my hand to wipe the wet off my lips. Just roll over to choke the pain pulsing from the arm that's stuck under my body. Just straighten out my leg . . . He must be lying right there, head on his paws, nose to my nose, for me to feel his breath swirling through my skull like this. I open my eyes. A close-up of Crassus's eyes. Why are your pupils so big? Are you on something, scumbag? Bitch, quit it. Quit licking my neck. Okay, fine. Fine.

I wipe the wet off my lips and get up. It's dead quiet. Dark. Crassus rubs his head on my shoes and whimpers. I sink my hand into his fur.

"What, hungry?"

He whimpers.

"Me too."

I follow Crassus off the side street and into the square. It's completely empty.

"Where did everyone go?"

Mr. Qolam and the pineapple heads and the helicopters? Crassus circles my legs.

"Did you fall asleep too?"

There's total silence. Like no one was ever here . . . Shit, my backpack.

"Crassus, I'm sure I had my backpack under my head when I fell asleep? Okay, okay, you can stop whining. Of course someone took it."

The road's covered in shards of glass and makeshift crowbars pried from broken crates. Mr. Reza's shop and the mini-mart next door look like caves. With the security gates broken you can see all the way back. To the backs of their sore throats where the uvula's showing. *Open wide and say "ahhh."* Crassus sticks his nose into some empty boxes and wags his tail.

"Come on, crazy, there's nothing in there."

A hulking yellow cat jumps out of the box and screams in his face. Crassus jumps a half meter in the air then runs to dig his snout into the back of my knees.

"Pussy."

The cat sticks its tail up skewer-straight and glares at me pissed.

"What, you practically gave him a heart attack! Now don't you have somewhere to be?"

I go downhill back through the square. Crassus runs ahead. When we reach the newsstand he turns around back toward the cat and barks at the top of his lungs.

"You're really killing me with the heroics here . . ."

It's like they've sprinkled some sort of death tonic over the neighborhood around the square. Total silence. The shops are all empty. Even the taftoon bakery. Where the hell did the bakers go? What time is it? Why don't I ever know what time it is? My body aches. I mean, how long was I asleep? Half my body's still numb. I rub my bicep with the other hand. Can't feel a thing. I sit down on the bench by the bakery, pull a cigarette out of pocket #1003 of my cargos, and slip it between my lips.

"Bet you can't find a lighter now, boy."

Crassus jumps onto the cement bench and puts his head on my lap.

"What did I say."

I take a shitty green lighter out of my jacket pocket. A soulless flame trickles out.

"Pocketed it at Sara's. Have I got skills or have I got skills."

I inhale.

"Think she was holding out on me?"

Crassus lifts his head and lets out a half-assed yawn.

"You coming down too?"

I inhale. Tastes like poison.

"How do we really know how much was left in that box?"

He whimpers.

"You just don't get it. Addiction's not about making friends."

He closes his eyes.

"Maybe the whole damn thing was a sham. Maybe Siamak woke her up this morning, put a solid twelve grams in her palm, and *then* split."

He whimpers and sets his head back down on my lap.

"But Rahim, that sonofabitch . . ."

I inhale.

"Where did everyone go, you think?"

Crassus lifts his head and perks his ears.

"What?"

Thump-thump goes a heavy beat while tires scream on asphalt and then—*aooo!* Crassus howls and scuttles behind my knees. Smoke rises off the hood of a Prado that just rammed straight into a tree. The *thump-thump* and full-throttle bray of Mayhem's "Freezing Moon" spills out the windows.

You could set a bomb off in a Prado and the stereo wouldn't even wince. The driver's head hangs over the steering wheel. I open the door. His torso tips into my arms. Crassus barks. His buzzed head and face are all covered in blood. I grab him by the armpits and pull him out. Don't these things have airbags? Dude must've had them removed to install the speakers in order to feel this fucker's braying course through every internal and external organ of his upper and lower body. Crassus barks and circles but won't get too close.

"Chill out, he's not dead."

Seriously, what kind of jackass gets behind the wheel

barefoot wearing nothing but shorts and a tank? I lay him down on the ground. I put my ear to his chest. Sounds like something's there. Except with a beat that's more like *to be or not to be*. Tattoos of spiders and crabs and seven or eight other creepy-crawlies skitter across his biceps. The gash on his forehead is as thick as my finger and it's bubbling blood. Blood that is so fucking red. Now Crassus is sniffing at the man's feet.

"So you've toughened up, I see."

His hands start shaking. His legs stick out skewer-straight. His chest rises. His head slams back onto the pavement. His eyes go white. His jaw goes crooked. He shakes. I take his head in my lap. He shakes.

"Shhh, relax. Relax."

The head in my lap shakes. A pair of white eyes stares at me. Blood streams out of the gash on his forehead. His hands claw at the air. White foam bubbles out through his teeth. I lift his torso. I hold him tighter. I press my head to his head.

"Please oh please try to relax."

Now we're moving together. Our heads shake together. His shoulders make my shoulders shake. I weave his clawing fingers between my fingers. His shaking ripples through my body. Rips through my body. It's like the critters from his biceps are walking along my spine. They start at the very bottom and calmly pull themselves up. Mayhem wails. My eardrums shake. Like some wild animal—now the ground's shaking too. And the tires are shaking. And Mayhem's cries are shaking. And Crassus digs his head into my neck and shakes. The shattered glass on the street shakes. The broken crates shake. The crumpled newspapers shake.

His fingers and my fingers stay interlocked. Everything's calmed down. Crassus still has his face tucked into my neck, paws over his eyes. I pry my fingers from his fingers and gently place his head on the ground. His eyes are closed and the long lashes overlap. The white foam around his mouth is cakey. Like a fire truck just put out a fire in his mouth. The gash on his forehead stares at me like an eye wide-open. The scorpions on his biceps stay where they belong. Mayhem brays.

Crassus sits next to me giving me Jean Reno eyes.

"Think Buzzcut's got any supplies in the car?"

If only Rahim were around. He'd know a thing or two about these metalheads, what they take, when they take it, where they take it—hell, Rahim would know where they keep the shit stashed. I open the dashboard. Mr. Whoopee's closet. Skulls and chains and voodoo dolls and a whole bunch of other shit spill out.

Under the seats.

Under the steering wheel.

Between the seat cushions.

By the stick shift.

Crassus looks at me sadly.

"Dammit, he already shot up his whole fucking supply."

I even go through his pockets. Nothing. Fuck you. Not even a cigarette?

"Hey, maybe this is the same loser who called Elham to put on that pathetic show."

Crassus throws himself into my arms.

"What, I say her name and you start pouting?"

He looks at me sadly.

"Seriously, maybe's it him. This dude definitely fucked up somehow, that's for sure. Then when the poor sucker's fuse ran short he got in the car."

I lean against Buzzcut's black Prado and light a cigarette. I need to think. Need to get my shit together. Need to figure out what kind of shit I need to get together. Why do I need to get my shit together? Can't I just lie here next to this corpse? Indeed I can. But what will I do in an hour when my nose starts running? Fuck all the fake friends in the world. Those spineless little shits. I sink my fingers into Crassus's fluff.

"Know what a fake friend is, Crassus?"

Buzzcut's sleeping so sound you'd think he's on a beach in the Canary Islands getting some sun as he waits for his girl to get back from her massage. Shit. Lucky you. Except I do wish I'd found that damn stash. Or maybe you're sober too? Maybe you also woke up this morning only to realize four of your spineless so-called friends had cleaned you out. Found that so un-fucking-believable you got behind the wheel and you've been spinning through the city all day trying to track down your dealers who have all melted straight into the ground.

Or maybe you're the one who copped your friends' shit and you were shooting up all day before you got behind the wheel to come down here and run into a tree and split your buzzed head open and pour your red red blood on the street and start shaking and foaming at the mouth . . . Okay, enough. Stop bullshitting. I grab Buzzcut by the armpits and drag him over to the car. The man's nothing but skin and bones. I open the back door and toss him onto the seat. Crassus doesn't make a peep. Or get any closer.

"What's up, Schwarzenegger, what's got you tied up in knots? Everything's just fine . . ."

Crassus stares at my hands. Fair. I look like a butcher who just slaughtered a cow.

"Aw, babe, there's nothing to be afraid of."

I hug his snout to my chest.

"It's Buzzcut's blood, not mine."

He nuzzles his snout into my neck.

"Hop in, let's go."

He hops into the car and sits in the passenger seat.

"As a great man once said, *Let's get out of here, fast as lightning.*"

I turn the ignition.

"Let's get out of here . . ."

I turn the ignition.

"Let's get . . . Let's—"

The car starts.

"Any idea how to put this thing in reverse?"

I push the stick shift all the way up and pull it into first. I hit the gas. The wheels spin in place and the bumper digs deeper into the tree.

"Oops, sorry!"

Well, my friend, looks like reverse is right where you left it. I dip the clutch and—voilà, the bumper stays stuck in the tree but we three back up. Turn the wheel and throw it in first and soon enough we're flying. Crassus puts his paws on the dashboard.

"Does the whole damn city look like this? Like a fucking ghost town? All the fucking cowards made a break for it?"

I put the pedal to the metal to cut the turns by Evin Prison. Downshift to second to get up the hill by the police station. Ghost-town Tehran makes you feel like a World Rally Champion. I take the roundabout by Shahid Beheshti and go up the boulevard. It looks so different with the lights off. Like it's giving us the silent treatment. I weave in and out of backstreets and alleyways. Take Thirteenth over to Borzoo and weave over to the top of Sa'dabad. Not a fly flies. If anyone's sticking around, it sure won't be the yuppies up here . . . Down by the old palace the road's blocked off. Riot cops surround the Sa'dabad police station like cartoon roaches forming a wall of flesh.

"Look, Crassus, not everyone made a break for it."

The road's blocked. I pull the emergency brake. Turn off the car. Buzzcut stays sound asleep. A stream of white foam runs from his mouth onto the seat cushion. But his face is calm and still. Calmer than calm. He probably sleeps a solid twenty-four hours after every epilepsy attack.

"That was a real dick move, dude, shooting it all up all by yourself."

I hop out. Crassus skips ahead and wags his tail acting cute again. He must've forgotten all about being hungry.

A few shiny green taxis are lined up nice and neat like a toy train. The drivers are sitting on the hoods of their cars, swinging their feet and snacking on seeds. One of them gives me a dark look. Shit, my hands. I step into the gutter and wash my hands in the water that trickles by. Now they're all looking at me, muttering. I make a pass at washing the front of my army jacket. Go ahead, stare until your eyes explode. I splash some water on my face. Crassus barks. He probably means the water isn't strictly sanitary. I pull my beanie down over my eyebrows and get going. I don't even glance at them.

Crassus stops in front of a cherry-red Paykan sports car. Either he's in love or he's caught a whiff of their food. The Paykan sits there with all four doors open. A man's feet hang off the edge of the back seat. A little girl sits behind the wheel swinging her pigtails and changing gears. A woman sits on a picnic blanket spread out by the tires. She's got her chador pinned up between her teeth and her nipple in the mouth of a toddler who glares at Crassus while sucking.

Crassus takes a seat at the edge of the blanket like a gentleman. He stares at the pot simmering on the propane burner. A second woman gets up and shoos him away. The man in the back seat rolls over. The woman throws a shoe in Crassus's face.

Crassus whimpers and sticks his snout into the back of my knees. The woman glares at me, turns her head, and mutters something. Okay, okay, chill. Crassus follows me out.

Sa'dabad Street is packed with Paykans and Prides

that are parked in the middle of the street with a picnic blanket spread out by the tires and kids crawling up the hoods and over the roofs. On the sidewalk in front of the mosque they've got thirty or forty guys handcuffed and on their knees. Riot cops stand at the gates rapping their batons against the railing. Every now and then they yell at the boys to quit squirming and sniveling. I want to go check it out—maybe Rahim or Siamak's in there—but I don't dare. I mean, if they are actually in there then I'm really screwed. What, now you want to play savior? Because the cops are definitely going to listen to you and set them free. And then surely on account of your kindness Rahim and Siamak will reach into their pockets and ta-da! a solid twenty-five grams. Bitch, get real. Fine. They'll fork up about half. Won't they?

People sit scattered all over Tajrish Square. On the lawn, in the street, on the sidewalk. Just like Sizdah Bedar. Let the good times roll. A herd of seven- or eight-year-olds is running around screaming on the lawn. Their mothers yell at them while stirring whatever's on the stove. The kids chase each other. They scream, they laugh, they scream. The fathers stand on the sidewalk and smoke. A general frowns as he holds forth. The fathers shake their heads. The general says something in his walkie-talkie and frowns again. The fathers shake their heads and take deep drags of their cigarettes. Crassus runs after the kids and barks.

"Get back here!"

Crassus skips through the lawn all cute and grabs

some little girl's skirt by the teeth. A boy picks up a rock and throws it at him. Crassus whimpers.

"What did I say."

I hold him. He looks at them sadly. The boy looks back and frowns, another rock at the ready.

"Come on, it looks like there's something to eat over there."

At the turnoff toward Jafarabad, a shit ton of men and women and children are lined up in front of a set of buffet counters. Soldiers bend over to hand out packaged lavash bread. They've even put up a first-aid tent next to the food. A few floozies are standing in line with their mothers. Women take the disposable plates and run back to their picnic blankets.

"Look, Crassus, there's adas polo."

I get in line behind a fat woman who's stuffed her stomach into a skintight manteau. She turns and blows a bubble in my face until it pops.

"The men's line is over there."

I hug Crassus to my chest and stand behind a group of boys with spiky hair. One of them looks at me then looks at his friends and raises an eyebrow. They whisper in each other's ears and toss their glassy laughter into the air. Crassus whimpers. Four or five riot cops pace between the lines. The boys stand still and bow their heads. The cops glare at me and the boys. The boys take their plates and scram. A soldier sticks his oar of a spatula into the pot and piles lentils and rice onto a plastic plate, the next one sets a couple dates on the side, the third one lays some bread on top and hands me the plate. I sit down in the crosswalk. Put the dates on the bread and roll it up like a sandwich. Crassus wags his tail and whimpers.

"Here, you mooch, all yours. I don't even like lentils."

I set the plastic plate in front of him and take a big bite from my date sandwich. It gets stuck in my throat. My mouth is dry. Dryer than dry. Between the boxwood hedges in the square a pretty boy's playing setar, singing hafez with his eyes closed. He's really feeling it.

"*Thinking myself an ascetic . . . ooo.*"

Four or five old men who look real chill are gathered around, swaying their heads and paying praise.

"*A fire-worshipper on every side, aahh . . .*"

"Bravo, bravo!"

The old men sing along softly with their eyes closed. One of them keeps lifting the lid off a teapot to look inside.

"A cup of tea to ease the dear boy's throat!"

The one who's messing with the teapot nods his head as in *my pleasure*. If only they'd give me a cup of tea. Pretty Boy plays flamenco guitar, thumb running up and down the strings. He frowns and belts it out from the bottom of his heart.

"*Ooo, aahh . . . I drum the daf and strum the harp.*"

Crassus slurp-slurps, with his snout digging into the plate like the famine just ended.

"Think they'd give me a cup of tea?"

He's not listening.

"I mean, I know I'm not as pretty."

I go squat down by their setup. The spindly old man

by the stove fills plastic cups with tea and the old man next to him passes them down without missing a beat. The little boys playing chase circle the old men's stuff and scream and shout. Someone gets up, yells at the kids, and shoos them away. Then lands a butt-slap on the last kid in reach for good measure. Perfect, I just need to nab him before he sits down again.

"Excuse me, could I bother you for a cup of tea?"

The old man frowns and scans me over head to toe. He's bent over with his hands above his knees. He looks at me suspiciously. This fucking screechy voice always gives a person away.

"Of course, son. Come, come."

I edge over and they make space for me. Cheers! They're fucking amazing.

"And one for our friend here."

I take the plastic cup. I should say thanks but I can't risk this nasally screech twice. The first old man squats down and drops a couple sugar cubes in my palm. The boy sings the last line of the ghazal and sets down the setar.

"Wonderful, wonderful."

"Take a bow!"

"Excellent, bravo!"

The maestro wipes the sweat off his brow and bows his head. Kudos to you. What humility, what a gentleman! If I had my violin on me I'd teach you a lesson. Hit that schnoz so hard . . . Take you down a notch. Bat those lashes a little harder, will you. Seriously? Reeling in a few old men doesn't warrant all that blushing.

"Pass the gentleman another tea."

You have got to be shitting me. I always have the worst luck. Watch them pass him a couple balls to top it off. Actually, getting a little friendly with these old fogies isn't such a bad idea. It just may be my deliverance. I take a pack of cigarettes out of pocket #206 of my cargos and hold it out. The old man takes one cigarette to tuck behind his ear and another to slip between his lips. I take one too and slip it between my lips. Now a light. A fucking light. Crassus, a light! I pat my pockets down. The old man lights a match. I lean over with my cigarette and bump fists in a *here's to you* kind of way. He takes a good long drag, narrows his eyes, and stares at me. This is when the questions start, then I suppose he'll want to give me some advice and tell me to go back home to my mother. Or who knows, maybe he's chill. The earth slips out from under my feet and I fall straight on my ass. The lights go off. The tremors rip through my body. Crassus howls. Loud, deep shouts come through the police megaphone:

"There is nothing to fear. Everything is under control. Do not panic."

The sound of screaming. The sound of supplications. The sound of heartbreaking cries. The sound of children wailing. The sound of women screaming. My eardrums are about to explode. The tremors ripple through my body. She makes her big fleshy breasts shake. She makes the rolls of her stomach shake and shakes the tips of her shoulders. She makes her whole body shake.

It's all over. All quiet. The lights around the square

turn back on. One of the old guys has fainted. The rest of them are gathered around, fanning him. Pretty Boy hugs his setar to his chest and chants . . .

"Siiiick. Hell yeah."

That's Arash's birdsong. Crassus perks his ears.

"Crassus, it's Arash!"

Crassus runs behind me. Arash is standing by the fish shop on the square, whistling with four fingers. I throw myself into his arms.

"Bitch, where have you been?"

I press my head into his chest. He smells like our childhood. Smells like his curly black hair. Smells like—he grabs me by the biceps, pulls me off of him, and gives me a shake.

"Bitch, you made a run for it or what. Bobak and Maman had their fingers up their asses in denial for a solid fifteen minutes."

I dig my head into his chest. Press my forehead into his rib cage.

"What's wrong with you? All touchy-feely. Took your happy pills?"

"Arash!"

Crassus runs and throws himself into Arash's arms. Arash dives to the ground and wrestles him. Crassus licks his face. Arash takes Crassus's ear between his teeth and barks. Crassus licks Arash's hair.

"Gross . . . Wait, what's this bitch doing here?"

Miss Gelin rests her chin on her knee and shakes her head.

"She's been riding my ass all day."

The electricity's back. People praise the Lord.

"What's she doing here?" I ask.

"What was I supposed to do. She already had a funeral planned for poor Aqdas so I put her on the back of my bike to come see the show. But then she's really been freaking out ever since she saw them nab Nana Molouk. I think she thinks she's next."

"So you saw that too?"

"Fuck yeah."

"Did you see what she was wearing?"

"It's mine. No idea when she swiped it."

"Think she's okay?"

"Yeah, dude, she and the rest of her crazy-ass friends are in there having a fucking ball."

I sit down next to Miss Gelin on the step.

"Are you okay?"

She shakes her head.

"Allah bilur Allah bilur."

She won't look at me. She's got her eyes glued to a faraway spot on the wall.

"Niyə mənə özünən aparmiyip."

"Who?"

"Khanum!"

"Yeah, she'll be back. She'll be back when she finds him, don't worry."

She shakes her head.

"Allah bilur Allah bilur."

A small bundle of her stuff sits by her feet. Her big floral scarf has slipped back past the crown of her head and her salt-and-henna hair falls over her sunken cheeks. She puts her chin on her knee and shakes her head.

"Allah bilur Allah bilur."

"Yeah. God knows."

Arash sits down next to me. Crassus is sprawled out on top of Arash, licking his face.

"Were you at Elham and them's?"

"Yeah."

I take a cigarette out of pocket #206 of my cargos.

"They doing okay? What're they up to?"

I use his barbecue lighter for a light.

"Yeah . . ."

I inhale.

"What's Ashkan up to?"

I inhale then let the smoke out through my nose.

"Killing himself."

He wets a joint on the tip of his tongue.

"How?"

"ODing on opium."

He lights it and takes a deep drag. Half the joint goes red.

"Did he die?"

I inhale.

"I don't know."

Arash passes me the joint. I pass him the cigarette. I inhale. He inhales. I hold in the smoke.

"What's Elham up to?"

I let it out.

"I don't know. She wasn't there."

I take a deep drag. The smell of weed swirls through my skull.

"But Parvin was having a good time. She was up there on the roof of the herb peddler's truck chanting into the mic."

"Good for her."

I pass the joint.

"Filter's too thin. Way too thin."

"Shut the fuck up."

He gets up. Crassus rolls onto the ground. His eyes are closed—he's still asleep.

"Something to eat, something to smoke, man, you must be floating now."

Crassus yawns and rests his snout on his paws. Arash comes back with a brush and a bucket of paint.

"I'm redoing the walls. Plus I found this fine specimen of a chaise. Putting it right here, baby, then I'm rolling up the gate and—lookout deluxe!"

"Here? Rotten fish smells good to you?"

"Focus. A decent coat of this sick color on the tiles over here, set the sofa over there . . ."

"Right."

"What you get is the view, windows on all four sides."

"What're you trying to do exactly?"

"Shit! Welcome to my new office. The view is everything."

"Right. And what business will you be conducting in this fine business establishment?"

"Good one. Well, I just stretch out on this here chaise—"

He saunters over, stretches out on the ratty green leather chaise, crosses his ankles, and folds his arms over his chest.

"—and watch the people go by."

He takes another joint out of the pocket of his safety vest, wets it with his tongue, and lights it.

"I've got ideas. Still working out the details."

"Impressive, truly . . . Say, you wouldn't know if Amu Mamdal and them stuck around, would you?"

He throws his laughter in my face along with a rush of smoke.

"Ha. Ha. Ha," I say.

"So Rahim and Siamak left you high and dry?"

"Fuck you."

He comes over, sits down next to me, and gives me a punch on the bicep.

"You never listen. I keep telling you to forget about those losers. This town's fucking flooded with dealers."

Crassus pokes his snout out of Arash's arms then tucks himself back in.

"They didn't give you anything?"

"They're not even around. Vanished in the middle of the night, both of them."

This time he claps and whistles as he snickers.

"Damn, that's good. Abadanis, authenticity guaranteed."

Crassus gets up, drags himself over to my lap in a sleepy haze, and yawns.

"You mean they screwed Shahnaz and Sara over too?"

"I don't know. I think so. I mean, Shahnaz was definitely losing it. But Sara I'm not so sure. Maybe she had more than she let on."

"Wow. Thanks, Sara, thanks a million."

"Amu Asodallah and them wouldn't split, would they?"

Arash frowns. He takes a hit and half the joint goes red. He sucks the air in through his teeth and holds it in his chest.

"Bitch, you seriously think that motherfucker would stick around?"

"Well yeah, why not?"

He blows the smoke in my face.

"Cause all the motherfucking cowards and little shits already made a break for it. You still don't get it, do you?"

He puts a hand in his pocket and takes out a small bottle of pills.

"Come and get 'em."

He sets the bottle in my palm.

"Watch you don't end up on Mars."

I take the bottle and open the lid. Little white pills.

"What is this?"

"Shiiit."

He leaves me on the step and goes over to plant his big ass back on the chaise.

"I fucking hate it when you put on airs. What difference does it make? You want to walk on the clouds, who fucking cares how you get there?"

Crassus is snoring. I get up and lay him on Arash's chest. He opens his eyes a sliver and looks at me.

"Shh, go back to sleep."

Arash hands me the joint. I take a puff and hand it back.

"That's the saddest excuse for a drag I've ever seen."

I hold in the smoke. Arash narrows his eyes and sucks in through his teeth, the air along with the smoke.

Miss Gelin's asleep, legs tucked in to her chest, head on her bundle. Arash gets up and runs to the back of the store. Whistling "O Fortuna." Sounds like a hose over a—I head out. Arash yells, "Where you going?"

"I'll be right back. Right back . . ."

The soldiers and cops are standing by their cars nodding off. The women and children are asleep on their picnic blankets mouths open. The men are sprawled out on the grass snoring. I climb down the cement slopes of the old riverbank. The smell of rotten trash swirls through my skull. The sewer down past the square is the perfect spot. No one'll find me here. Definitely not Arash, rats scare him shitless . . . I lie down. I take the unlabeled pill bottle in my palm. Seriously, what difference does it make? What matters is getting the little creature to crawl up my spine. But these pills are really little. White and little. I pour them out into my palm. How many did Arash say it takes to get to Mars? I pour them back into the bottle. Put just two under my tongue. Shut my eyes and swallow the bitterness. The bitterness goes down. The little creature comes up through my legs and leaps into my stomach. Explodes into a thousand pieces, pieces that wiggle in my stomach and cascade down my legs and swim through my veins like tadpoles. The tadpoles go down and then pull themselves back up and release themselves into my pelvis, a thousand of them rushing down a channel into a single little swamp. Now they're swimming through my stomach. I suck. That's right. I won't go all the way to Mars. Just up. Up in the air. And if I come down before cashing in I can just pop another two, and then—a cry sounds from somewhere far away. A deep, tired voice singing something like folk songs. No. It doesn't sing the songs, it cries them. I suck and push the bitterness down.

Translator's Note

Mahsa Mohebali's *In Case of Emergency* (originally *Nigarān nabāsh*, or literally "Don't worry") made a splash in Tehran when it was first published in 2008, receiving, among other accolades, a Hooshang Golshiri Literary Award (comparable to a Pulitzer). Imagining an apocalyptic day of earthquakes in Tehran, the novel follows Shadi through a single day as she copes with her rich, dysfunctional family, roams through the city's chaotic streets, and visits various friends who are more or less as depressed and aimless and addicted as she is—all in search of her next fix. The voice is as consistently insouciant as its original and translated titles suggest, platitudes and empty warnings that must be read flatly and sarcastically, small consolations in the face of a crumbling world. Indeed, the novel was celebrated for shamelessly portraying an uncouth patois and subculture not typically permitted on the page, whether censored by author- and reader-inscribed rules of respectability or by the Ministry of Culture. It's a marvel it ever got a permit for publication, but it did; and in the decade since, it has been on and off the shelves, a dozen or so print runs bleeding through a start-and-stop game of censorship.

For well over a century, if not two, European-language translation has been tied up in the domestication versus foreignization debate: Does the translator bring the text to readers, performing a process of adaptation, or does she bring readers to the world of the text, encouraging them to respect its customs, at best, or exoticizing it, at worst? In the past few decades, these debates have taken a postcolonial turn. In translation from the Global South especially, domestication is deemed a violence that erases difference and privileges Western cultural modes. Yet in translating a contemporary cult classic from Iran, I have staked the opposite claim: because modern Iran is regarded as alien, let alone foreign, by the US and Western Anglophone world, domestication can in fact serve to deeply discomfit the reader, forcing "him"—the masculine pronoun is significant here, for gendered forms of power are at play—to confront the other's humanity.

As a translator I have tried to breathe new life into this text, aiming to re-create the naturalism of the original text in an International English–inflected dialect with an American idiom at its core.

In the spirit of Susan Bernofsky's strategy of "turning up the volume" on a translation to preserve style,[1] not to mention voice, I have enabled Shadi and her peers to curse more freely than her original censors would allow. More "respectable" characters like Shadi's mother and older brother, Bobak, keep to the R-passing-as-PG-13 tone of the original, favoring light curse words like "damn" and "goddamn" over "fuck" and its variants. In early drafts I translated the entire text this way, shying away from "fuck." But Shadi sounded dorky. I had successfully quashed her cool, effectively censoring the text a second time. In consulting with the author, I decided to let her English avatar breathe. Now everyone drops the "f-bomb" whenever seems natural—which is a lot.

Even so, the radicalism of the original can hardly be translated into American English. For to print, in Tehran, the cursing and slang that appear in the Farsi original—words that I, for one, could never utter at my parents' table, no matter what Shadi seems to get away with—makes a louder statement than any English text, however riddled with profanity, could ever make in the US. In the US, the history of a free press means that censorship usually takes more subtle forms, including through adjudicating what "counts" as literature: not the state's red pen but the black ink of publishing contracts dictates what we read as Americans, whether in translation or otherwise. Perhaps here as in Iran, a novel like *In Case of Emergency* is as much a "fuck you" to canonized literature and ideas of literariness as it is a love note to those same institutions and ideals.

The novel's conceit, Shadi's addiction to drugs and the withdrawal that motivates her daylong odyssey, is a major public health issue in Iran. In 2005, around the time of Mohebali's writing, narcotics sales in Iran were estimated at $10 billion, and 2.8 percent of the population between ages fifteen and sixty-four used illegal drugs, so that Iran had the highest per capita opiate use in the world.[2] But I would argue that, in the novel, drug use also constitutes a politics of refusal: the refusal to work and love—both family and friends—in the usual ways.

An earthquake apocalypse might similarly be taken both literally and figuratively. Iran is situated on a major fault line, and the novel exploits this physical instability as a metaphor for the threat of social unraveling that hangs over the country. Indeed, in this text there is no small dose of political critique mixed into the fun (and funniness). For example, a careful reader will notice that when Shadi gets dressed to leave the house in chapter 2, she puts on a skullcap but no scarf. In Iran today, some women cross-dress as men to circumvent mandatory public veiling, a relatively common form of civil disobedience given its great risk. Alongside Shadi's masculinity, there is too the femininity of male characters like Ponytail and the protesting "gays" Shadi sees on the streets in chapter 6. Thus, gender-bending figures in this novel as a politics in the strictest and broadest senses, redefining the individual's relationship to both the state and the social and defying those norms. Translated into a US American context, one might call this politics queer.

But then what to do with the anti-queer—and specifically anti-trans—sentiment bubbling under the surface, also in chapter 6, when Ponytail alludes to Shadi's cross-dressing by remarking on her hat? "So what's the deal," he asks her on page 82 of the current translation, "you some sort of crisscrosser or something?"

What now appears as "crisscrosser" reads as *tiransfir-miransfir* in the original, combining a transliteration of the English "transfer" that hints at transness with a nonsense diminutive (much more common in spoken Farsi, this construction works something like the phrase "easy peasy"). Trans folks in Iran do not self-identify as *tiransfir*s. Ponytail, in short, doesn't know what he's talking about, and the additional diminutive means he's far from an ally. Thus I could not in good conscience translate the question as "So what's the deal, you trans or something?" That would be giving Ponytail too much credit, sanitizing the text. I am of the belief that we must confront forms of difference-making like anti-transness, homophobia, and racialization head-on if we are to work against it. Yet using a known English slur was uncalled for: Ponytail is confused but not malicious, and neither is the novel. After a year or more of circling this issue, I finally decided on the neologism "crisscrosser," which gets at the idea of crossing binaries, as does the prefix "trans-," but does not quite get it right. In lieu of a diminutive, the phrase "or something" then adds that edge of ignorance Ponytail sadly betrays.

On the other hand, I find that in Farsi gendered curse words do not map quite as cleanly onto gender-"appropriate" subjects—or if they do in Farsi, then at least not in this gender-bending book. Straightening the text was out of the question, even more so given the significance of cross-dressing in this novel. Thus I have had Shadi apply "bitch" to any number of male characters, including to the elderly landlord, the Colonel, in chapter 5, where an English speaker might expect a masculinized curse word such as "asshole." These crossed vectors are meant to signal the reader not to take the feminine gendering of "bitch" elsewhere too seriously, and certainly not as anti-feminist. When passed between Shadi and Sara in chapter 7 as a translation for any number of teasing insults such as *kisāfat* and *'avazī*, "bitch" becomes a pet name charged with female homoeroticism. Of course the queer use of "bitch" in English today as alternately an insult and a term of endearment helps my case.

An Anglophone reader will be struck—and perhaps even snag on—the repetition that riddles this text literally and structurally, in stock phrases, in recurring images, and syntactically. Whereas English literary norms regard repetition as lazy and lowly, repetition is well respected in the Farsi canon, perhaps because of the way couplets historically lean on conjugated verbs for easy rhymes (in formal Farsi, the verb comes last). I have kept thematically meaningful repetition but also allowed the text to live in English. English has a particularly broad vocabulary, and in verbs especially. I have taken pleasure in this abundance to variously translate into English the same word or phrase in Farsi unless significant. In chapter 1, for example, Shadi's brother, Arash, uses the phrase *zadan bih chāk*—literally, "to hit the split"—to say that their grandmother, Nana Molouk, has left the house; he then repeats the idiom in chapter 2 to say that all the "motherfucking cowards" are leaving town. In the former case, I take advantage of the resonances between the literal translation of "hitting the split" and "splitting" in everyday English, while in the latter I use a different idiom altogether, "to make a break for it."

That English and Farsi are both so idiomatic can make it difficult to move between them. At times, for the sake of style and tone, I avail myself of an English idiom when the original is more straightforward. The seemingly gratuitous use of "fucking" and "motherfucking" as modifiers—as in "motherfucking cowards" above; in the original Arash simply says "cowards"—serves such a purpose, lending the dialogue authenticity in English. Which is also to say, the modifier "fucking" is not meaningful in contemporary English but idiomatic. But I never deploy an English idiom that is culturally inappropriate. When a little old lady "takes steps the size of a sparrow's" in chapter 3, I leave the Farsi as is, allowing that image to unobtrusively enter English, rather than relying on the more readily available "inches forward": Iran uses the metric system and even metaphoric inches have no place.

Humor has also offered the chance opportunity for translative flair. In chapter 3 Arash accuses Shadi of "shoving her pills up the wrong hole," a jab that in a more innocent world I might have translated as "waking up on the wrong side of the bed." In the strictest sense, the phrase as I have rendered it constitutes a mistranslation: the Farsi *pusht o rū*—"back over front," or "inside out"—suggests a topsy-turviness tamer than my crass rendition. But inasmuch as "inside out" both falls flat and fails to carry Arash's voice, coming up with a better joke was the only way to accurately translate Arash's character—and I'd like to think the alternate Farsi interpretation, "back *over* front," slides easily into "back *to* front," which is, after all, but a baby step away from "up the wrong hole." In translating humor, one has to go far to get close.

Almost all references literary, musical, and filmic are in the original, including that to Agatha Christie's Miss Marple and that to the fumbling character of Mr. Whoopee in the 1960s cartoon *Tennessee Tuxedo and His Tales*. In chapter 3, however, I embellish the word "wretched" (*bīchārih*) as "the wretched of the earth," inserting a reference to Fanon in order to demonstrate Shadi's critical intellectualism, where song lyrics from an Iranian indie rock musician such as Soheil Nafisi in the same chapter will fail to land for the unfamiliar reader. I thus aim to translate milieu as well as text.

To that end I will note that the novel's "soundtrack," which ranges from soulful tunes by Tom Waits and Soheil Nafisi and Mohsen Namjoo to metal by Mayhem to classical compositions by Mozart and Bach, and which is available as an appended playlist at the back of the book, is in the original a true "Western-Eastern" hybrid, a Goethean feat. At several points Shadi's narration interweaves contemporary lyrics. Where Farsi lyrics were concerned, I squeezed and hacked at the translated lines to make them "musical," inserting rhyme and meter. But quotes of Waits and Mayhem that appeared in English in the original had to go due to copyright, so that the current text falsely stresses indigenous voices where the original blended Iranian and American, Western and Eastern.

Lyrics taken from Hafez ghazals, a common feature of traditional Iranian music and thus, too, of contemporary compositions that play with such forms, became an albatross around my neck. Note that Nima Yushij's modern verse also makes its way into the novel by way of song lyrics (in chapter 3), challenge enough in the midst of developing a prose style in translation—but casually translating Hafez remains a singular task. Chapter 5 presents parts of Hafez 417 and 418, while chapter 9 borrows from Hafez 296. A hemistich here and another there, such snippets are recognizable to an educated Iranian audience; curtailed and served to an Anglophone audience that cannot take their Sufi-inflected vocabulary for granted, however, Hafez's playful lines seem even more confusing. To curb such frustration, I worked from the original ghazals, rendering as much of each quoted line as seemed necessary to get the gist. I then tweaked them to produce precisely that cheesiness Shadi so despises in Iranian indie music, peppering the lines with easy rhymes and a sense of melodrama. In short, this "Hafez" is workable only in the context of this book. Don't let my hacked-up, hackneyed renditions scare you off from the old Shirazi poet; taken seriously, Hafez shines.

Translating transliterated English from the Farsi

back into English (such as *tiransfir*, above) posed another grand challenge. Simply leaving these phrases as English flattens the text and erases its multilingualism. To counter this, I inserted multilingual words and phrases when opportunities organically arose. Inasmuch as a command of English places Shadi and her family in the Iranian upper crust—English is not taught in public school but rather requires private instruction—I have relied on some light French and Latin to suggest such class distinctions in English. Examples include "sou" instead of "penny" for the small coin "qirān," long out of circulation and idiomatically referenced in chapter 2, as well as the foreshortened "*Et tu Brute?*" in chapter 7, when Shadi questions her loyalties to her old friend Sara. Otherwise Shadi commands herself to get it together with terms like "forza" and "yallah," though I kept the untranslated Farsi prayer-cum-rallying cry "ya abolfazl" in chapter 1 for flavor.

Miss Gelin's Azeri Turkish appears as it was in the original, untranslated and in the appropriate sister script (here in modified Latin, originally in Perso-Arabic). Shadi and her family can understand the maid's Azeri in the same way a rich kid might understand Spanish due to the nanny, but most Iranian readers, like American readers, and like me—I had to have these portions of dialogue translated for me and the alphabet checked—will be lost, relying on Shadi's half of the conversation to glean the whole. The sexually climactic *ich komme* ("I'm coming") is also in the original, a nod to the prevalence of German porn in Tehran, I'm told. Incidentally I once asked a friend familiar with the Iranian context whether they had any theories as to why or how this book could ever get published. They figured the censor assigned to the case was so distracted by form he forgot about content. And surely a few tricks like this could not have hurt.

All in all, the text's international purview reflects Iran's place in the global contemporary, which is more centered than popular American media might have it. *In Case of Emergency* offers a critique much bigger than that bounded by postrevolutionary Iran: it wages a war against respectability politics and the very idea of an individual's productive responsibility, a cross-cultural value upon which global capital depends. Through localized protest, globalized gender and sexuality come under scrutiny. The story asserts the right to flirt with, if not to fuck—and fuck with, and fuck up—whomever and whatever one wants, whenever one wants. This translatable and relatable message is, as I see it, an anti-credo the novel offers us as readers and citizens of today's world.

—Mariam Rahmani

Notes

1. Susan Bernofsky, "Translation and the Art of Revision," in *In Translation: Translators on Their Work and What It Means*, eds. Esther Allen and Susan Bernofsky (New York: Columbia University Press, 2013), 223–33. See 230–31.

2. Janet Afary, *Sexual Politics in Modern Iran* (Cambridge, UK: Cambridge University Press, 2009), 365; Roxanne Varzi, "A Grave State: Rakhshan Bani-Etemad's *Mainline*," in *Iranian Cinema in a Global Context: Policy, Politics, and Form*, eds. Peter Decherney and Blake Atwood (New York: Routledge, 2018), 96–111. See 97 and corresponding footnotes on 108. The oft-quoted figure of 2.8 percent is reported in the United Nations Office on Drugs and Crime's 2008 World Drug Report available online at www.unodc.org.

Playlist

CHAPTER 2: Niccolò Paganini, unnamed duet
Wolfgang Amadeus Mozart, Sonata no. 1

CHAPTER 3: Mohsen Namjoo, "Jabr" ("Algebra")
Tom Waits, "Christmas Card from a Hooker in Minneapolis"
Reza Sadeghi, "Vaysa Donya"
Soheil Nafisi, "Ay Adamha" ("Oh Humans") (lyrics taken from an eponymous Nima Yushij poem)

CHAPTER 5: Mohsen Namjoo, "Chashmi o sad nam" (lyrics taken from famous Hafez ghazals, combining Hafez 417 and 418)

CHAPTER 7: Johann Sebastian Bach, Invention no. 8
Unnamed Armenian folksong

CHAPTER 8: Johann Sebastian Bach, Mass in B Minor

CHAPTER 9: Mayhem, "Freezing Moon"
Mansour, "Bezan Berem"
Unrecorded folk rendering of Hafez ghazal 296

THE FEMINIST PRESS
AT THE CITY UNIVERSITY OF NEW YORK
FEMINISTPRESS.ORG

Praise for
Finding Your Third Place

"Rick Kyte's insight into the vital human experience of connection and friendship is both scholarly and inspiring. The next time I visit my favorite coffee shop, I'm leaving my laptop at home. It's time to look outward and engage more fully with others in our third places."

—Amy Dickinson, "Ask Amy" advice columnist and author of *The Mighty Queens of Freeville*

"Rick Kyte's plea to find a place in our lives for friendship could not be more timely. He weaves together storytelling, literature, and empirical evidence in a book that reminds us that simple fellowship is the first step to solving many of the problems facing our communities and our world."

—Dr. Stephanie A. Urchick,
Rotary International President, 2024–2025

"Wise, informative, helpful. *Finding Your Third Place* offers an amazing blend of science, art, and philosophy that at the same time educates, uplifts, and inspires you to reach out and help someone who may be feeling lonely today. During the present times when our 'society is meeting all our needs except that of friendships,' Rick Kyte's work and insights are timeless and much needed, both at work and in personal life."

—Dr. Amit Sood, author of *Mindfulness Redesigned* and *The Mayo Clinic Guide to Stress-Free Living*

"In *Finding Your Third Place*, Rick Kyte rekindles 'the feelings that make the town' of which Socrates spoke so long ago. Kyte's symposium is a modern homage to friendship and love. In this wonderful book, he sees our modern world through the eyes of ancient classical wisdom, and that helps us see ourselves anew, giving us new understanding of who we are and what we need for abundant human life. Kyte interweaves stories of everyday life with ancient wisdom to bring home powerful timeless truths about the importance of love, friendship, and community that will change us and the way we see the world forever."

—Jim Bailey, MD, Benjamin Franklin Award–winning author of *The End of Healing*

"Kyte shows us the essential role of third places, like an underground aquifer that allows the flourishing of all. *Finding Your Third Place* is about finding ourselves, finding the taproot of a common life, finding the very foundations of being human, together."

—Dr. Amy Oden, Adjunct Professor of Early Church History and Spirituality, St. Paul School of Theology; author of *Right Here, Right Now: The Practice of Christian Mindfulness*

"Rick Kyte offers a timely call for the kind of institutions we most need to create solidarity in a time of growing polarization and loneliness. Third places are where 'strangers can become acquaintances.' They are essential institutions for Tocquevillian democracy. Very fitting for a book that began in a coffeehouse called Common Grounds."

—Beau Weston,
Van Winkle Professor of Sociology, Centre College

"As Rick Kyte observes, 'It is in conversation that we find belonging.' Read this lovely, thoughtful book and then go out and engage. With someone, anyone—whether it's a cherished old friend who needs you at a dire moment, or a complete stranger who is searching for a light in life—wherever it is that you connect. It will help you. It will help them. And that help will cascade in crucial ways that will fill you with joy and purpose."

—Lisa Napoli, Author of *Ray and Joan* and *Radio Shangri-La*

"'Only connect!' the British writer E. M. Forster implored more than a century ago in his novel *Howard's End*. 'Live in fragments no longer.' In *Finding Your Third Place*, ethicist Rick Kyte follows Forster's instruction, exploring the roots and consequences of our modern crisis of loneliness. Kyte invites us to see through our superficial hyper-connectivity, and to reclaim the real spaces in our lives and landscapes where affection may again create coherence, meaning, and shared values."

—Curt Meine, Author of *Aldo Leopold: His Life and Work*

"This book will challenge readers to rethink how our lives and communities have been arranged for efficiency and the impact that has had on not only our individual social and emotional well-being, but also the health of our communities. Third places are the antidote for isolation."

—Beth Hartung, Owner of Pearl Street Books